WILD PITCH

A. B. Guthrie, Jr.

BANTAM BOOKS

TORONTO · NEW YORK · LONDON · SYDNEY · AUCKLAND

WILD PITCH

*A Bantam Book / published by arrangement with
Houghton Mifflin Company*

PRINTING HISTORY
*Houghton Mifflin edition published 1973
Bantam edition / August 1987*

ISBN 0-553-26719-1

Published simultaneously in the United States and Canada

PRINTED IN THE UNITED STATES OF AMERICA

KR   0 9 8 7 6 5 4 3 2 1

MURDER IN MONTANA

Back on the crest of the ridge, Charleston moved from one place to another, his eyes on the ground. I didn't know what he looked for until he said, "Jase, it's damn unlikely it was any kind of automatic, which would eject the casing itself, but isn't it likely that a man used to guns would work the lever or pump without thinking? Unless, of course, he'd thought about that."

We scuffed through the grass and examined the gravel without results, and then got back in the car.

"Now," the sheriff told me when we were rolling again, "we'll drop in to pass the time of day with Mr. Ben Day."

I spoke the thought that came to me. "Mr. Charleston, excuse me, but oughtn't you be armed?"

He turned long enough to grin at me and answer, "My cause is just."

Other books by A. B. Guthrie, Jr.

Arfive

The Big Sky

Fair Land, Fair Land

The Last Valley

These Thousand Hills

The Way West

To my children
Bert and Helen
and with thanks to
Charles J. Katz, M.D.

AUTHOR'S NOTE

People come in all shapes and sizes, it has been said, and so, somewhere in this world, someone may find a resemblance to himself in one of my characters; but I do not know, have not met, and never have heard about this possible counterpart.

A. B. G., Jr.

CHAPTER ONE

I was squeezing a baseball when a shirttail character named Lancaster banged into the sheriff's office to report what he said was a murder. For reasons other than alliteration we called him Loose Lip or Loose for short. The old wall clock that I wound once a week said the time was 11:30 P.M.

"By God, Chick, by God, a shootin', a downright murder! A damn murderer on the loose! Buster Hogue, that's who. And there at the annual picnic."

Chick Charleston answered, "Easy." He was an easy man, mostly, that is. "Now who and what?"

"Buster Hogue, I told you."

"Shot or shooter?"

"The shooter shot him, like I been sayin'. In the head. Smack in the bald spot."

"Sit down, Loose. One thing at a time. Where, now?"

"In his head. Oh, there on that little flat on the river. You know. Where we picnic every year, us that lives in the canyon and roundabout there. You've seen it, fishin'. Mouth of the canyon. You comin'?"

The sheriff leaned back in his chair. I found I was still squeezing the baseball, though the reason seemed pretty remote.

"Who fired? Was there a fight?"

"Hell, no, no fight. It was a picnic."

"Yeah, a picnic." The sheriff sat a little more forward, as if the movement might bring some order into Lancaster's report. "Who did it?"

"Would I be here if we knew? Wouldn't I be

1

helpin' with a rope? It was a shot out of the dark, and that's where you come in, to find out. That's what taxes are for."

Loose's taxes, I happened to know, were delinquent, what little they were.

"Is Buster Hogue dead?"

"As good as. What do you expect with a bullet in your bean?"

"Where is he now?"

"Loaded on a truck and comin' in slow. The boys rigged a litter for him. Got to go easy on account of that rocky-ass road, though Buster ain't feelin' nothin'."

"All right. Now let's start from the first."

"Chick, you ain't listenin'. I done told you. All this palaver, and you might be corralin' that bushwhacker." Loose flung a wave toward me. "And here's that pitcher of yours just feelin' a ball."

"Just tell me. All of it."

"It was a good night for it, for the picnic, I mean. Moonlight as all hell. We even shot at a mark, some of us, and done fine. That's how bright. Maybe forty or so of us there, countin famblies and guests. A bottle or two had went 'round, like they do. After we had target practiced and drunk and et, we set around the fire. There was some singin'. Buster, I happened to take note, had took off his hat."

"You wouldn't know whether everybody was there. All the time? When the shot was fired?"

"Some was roamin' around, I guess. Don't ask me who. And some probably had to go off in the bushes, after drinkin' and stuffin' theirselves."

"No one saw the shot, I take it. No one saw the sniper, even in the moonlight?"

"Not so's you'd notice. Might have been up on a ridge, or behind a bush or jack pine or all three. It was plumb lucky—or likely it won't do no final good—that Doctor Ulysses Pierpont was there."

"He's that psychiatrist?"

"I guess so. Head doctor, they say, and Buster was shot in the head. He wrapped up Buster's skull and said it looked serious, the doctor did."

"He coming along to town?"

"No. He said he'd done all he could, which was plenty good, way I saw it. He sure shooed that professor away, him that was first tryin' to help Buster."

"Who?"

"Hawthorne, that's his name. Professor Hawthorne. Kind of a newcomer. But, Christ sake, shake a leg, Chick!"

"We'll wait for the truck," Charleston said.

"Wait!" Loose's tone had gone shrill.

"Wait." The sheriff's one word, spoken as it was, snubbed Loose up, like a fretful horse to a post. "But I'll alert Old Doc Yak."

Old Doc Yak wasn't the right name of the town's only doctor. Old-timers, remembering a past-and-gone cartoon character, had nicknamed him that, and the nickname had buried the real one. I couldn't see that that aged and rickety pill-prescriber could help much. He wasn't a surgeon: he was a homeopath, which itself is something apart from the common-run healers.

While the sheriff called and as we waited, I had time to think about Buster Hogue. Years ago, I knew from report, he had started out with just about one cow and one acre of land. By one means or another—hard work he always said, not without truth—he had built that first stake to maybe fifteen thousand acres, not counting leased land, and a herd of cattle too big for more than loose estimate. And he still was expanding, or had been.

He was land-hungry but a far shot from land-poor. Along the way he had picked up plots, quarter sections, sections and more, being in a preferred spot because in the later years he had the cash ready. He was grass-hungry, too, which isn't quite a repetition of what's already been said. He liked the grass of his neighbors, or liked his cattle to feed on it. And so, on occasions fitting and proper, he left their gates open and let some of his cows through. Or so it was said. And it must have been true, else no one would have heard about altercations.

Hogue had always come out of these quarrels with

a whole hide—which was no wonder much. He was a combination of good nature, apology, bluster and toughness, and he could swing weight befitting the biggest rancher in the county. People as a whole rather admired him, more maybe for the mix of his talents than for the size of his roll. Even the wronged ones seemed to wind up resigned if still resentful. No one, I thought, could actively hate the old, fat son of a bitch, not really hate such a character. But now, it appeared, someone had.

We were waiting outside, me minus my baseball, when the truck pulled up. The sheriff directed it to Old Doc Yak's office. There four of us took hold of the litter and steered it inside. Buster Hogue wasn't dead yet: dead men didn't snore. After we had lifted the litter to a table, Doc Yak shooed us out, all but the sheriff.

Three men had come in with the truck—Guy Jamison, who owned it, Blue Piatt and Oscar Oliphant. The last two were crusty old-timers who had little places up toward the canyon. The world would have said they didn't amount to much. Guy Jamison, younger by a score or so of years, was a right man, who was establishing a dude ranch and outfitters' business four miles up in the mountains. We talked about the shooting and got nowhere beyond the bald fact of it.

The sheriff came out and announced after he had spotted me, "He's got a chance. The doctor says the bullet didn't break through the bone but fractured it plenty. We have to get him to the city. Jason"—that was me—"lacking an ambulance, I've begged the hearse off Felix Underwood. He doesn't want to drive that sixty miles to the hospital. Go get it, please." He looked around. "You, Terry, there. How about going with him?"

Terry Stephens said, "Sure thing." He was a friend of mine about my own age, which was seventeen.

So I fetched the hearse, and we gentled Buster Hogue in. Just as we were about to wheel off, Old Doc Yak scrambled out of his office and climbed into the corpse section alongside Buster, aiming if he could, I guessed, to see that the hearse didn't fulfill its true function during the trip. That was a thing you could say for the doc: he lived and died with his patients.

As we pulled away, the sheriff was beckoning to the other men to come with him.

It was a long drag to the city, but Terry and I didn't say much, both of us feeling ghostly, I supposed, in a machine that had taken so many men to the graveyard. There seemed to be the smell of old roses and wilting carnations in it and the vapors, the dust, of dreams come to an end. Or the faint, lingering spirits of ancient codgers and grandmas whose dreams died ahead of the flesh.

The downing moon was ghostly, too. At full blush a full moon seems to spin like a fixed top. This one, just over the mountains, had lost its whirl and was ready to topple. Its long, last rays, ahead and to the side of our headlights, made crazy, light-and-dark strangers of the humps and hollows and buttes and small groves that both of us knew. Shortened and elongated, cast out of shape, weird, they kept us company and shut up our mouths.

A couple of men in white helped us unload Buster at the hospital's emergency entrance. By his long, hoarse but regular breathing, you could tell he was quite a ways from dead yet. Doc Yak went inside for a while, came out and climbed in with us, and we set out for home.

CHAPTER TWO

I wasn't a deputy sheriff that summer when Buster Hogue got his skull cracked, or ever afterward for that matter. I was too young for a badge. What I was was a flunky, though the word didn't occur to me then. I served a few harmless papers, sat at the phone on occasion and ran errands, of which driving that old hearse with its unconscious cargo was the most important to date.

Old Jimmy Conner, who was deputized but served mostly as jailer, wouldn't have agreed with me as to what was of first importance. I saved his bum feet by trotting to the Commercial Cafe and bringing back grub for whatever guests he happened to be entertaining at the moment. The sheriff had two other deputies. One of them was assigned to the other end of the county, where a brash oil-field settlement had sprung up. The remaining member of the resident staff was Halvor Amussen.

Halvor was an oversized Norwegian or Swede or Dane and, in any case, all tomcat. He and old Jimmy had a way of switching around on day and night shifts so you never could be sure which one at which time would be on duty. No matter. One of them always was.

Besides being convenient for Halvor, the arrangement suited Jimmy all right. His wife was a practical nurse and hence a hit-and-miss homebody. Sometimes, for want of some place to go, Jimmy would hang around the office long after his shift. The circumstances, his and his wife's, seemed to make for a good marital relationship.

The county force was big enough, given my help, of course. Our town numbered only about 1500 souls and the county maybe 3500 or 4000 at the most.

Though I wasn't a deputy, I could still count myself a member of the crew, and every week Charleston paid me three to five dollars, depending. I thought the money came from the county. It didn't.

The job gave me pride. To be seen with Chick Charleston, who was Mister or Sheriff to me, gave me more. He looked like justice or law or clean order, and all of them tallied up. Habitually he wore polished boots and white, fitted shirts, often with a string tie, and a sand-colored stockman's hat and frontier jacket and pants. If anything was lacking in the picture, it was a holstered six-gun, which he seldom strapped on. But he moved with a smooth, thoughtful assurance, with an easy grace, natural to him, that in itself spoke authority.

Chick Charleston had drifted into town when I was in grade school and, for one reason or another, had stayed put, coasting along on an income or savings that people speculated about. He wasn't above being a good extra hand, though, when it came to branding or trailing cattle to and from summer range. His right name was Charles Charleston. "I guess," he explained to me once, smiling his open smile, "the old folks were so stuck on the sound of Charleston that they wanted to repeat it, even bobtailed."

His old folks, rumor had it, were among the descendants of the English and Scottish dudes who had staked out their cattle kingdoms in Wyoming and gone belly up in the mortal winter of 1886-87. Maybe so. He could talk our language, the loose, occupational language of the small western town, but he could also talk the language of a culture beyond most of us.

A strange gink, the town thought before it got used to him and accepted him as part of its pattern along with the judge and the banker, the wet-pants half-wit, who swamped the Bar Star Saloon, and old Mrs. Jenkins, who yelled hymns while ankling to and from the post office where she never got any mail.

Then, provoked beyond endurance one night, he thrashed Ben Day, an ex-con and born brawler and also owner of a run-down ranch, who had whipped every other man he could get to stand up to him. So Charleston's admirers put him up for sheriff, an office he didn't much want, and put him back in the courthouse four years later without opposition.

If I didn't know where my pay came from, I did know for sure that I was where I was because once I was a juvenile delinquent.

Some four years before, a friend and I had broken into a vacant country house to warm up after being caught in a blizzard while hunting ducks. Kindling and paper being right at hand, we built a fire in the old Cole's Hot Blast stove. Then, comfortable, we roamed the big house and happened on to pillows and began chasing and beating each other with them. The pillows were stuffed with feathers. At first, I mean. We tossed away the slack covers, found some soap and drew pictures on mirrors. My contribution to art was a naked man at the ready. My friend did even better.

And yet there was a kind of innocence in all we did. We didn't set out to do damage. We didn't aim to show off, or chagrin or embarrass anybody. We didn't give one thought to other people. It was as if the house, vacated, never again would be seen by human eyes. I doubt we even went that far in our thinking, if any. We were there, the house was there, and so—

It happened, though we didn't know it then, that my friend lost his bandanna during our frolic. It happened that a member of the family that owned the house found it. It happened that my friend's old man owned and operated the only laundry in town. From owner to sheriff to laundryman—and then our inning in court.

We were summoned from class, my friend and I, and led by our fathers to the office of old Judge LePage, who was only a justice of the peace but solemn enough for any and all jurisdictions. Ours was a silent and sorry walk, with guilt riding us and our fathers marching on either side, but sorrier yet was the time to come.

There were maybe a dozen men in the judge's little hearing room, all looking as if they never had strayed from the paths of righteousness since being signed up for the Sunday school cradle roll. They were stiff as set slabs of lutefisk, which is a dried fish that has to be soaked and lyed and otherwise treated before becoming unfit for human consumption.

All were like that but the sheriff, that is, the enemy who had exposed us. He sat in the front row, 175 pounds of law enforcement carefully dressed, and his face wore the look neither of censure nor triumph. I didn't know what to make of that look. Thoughtful? Impersonal? Coolly resigned to the fool ways of boys?

Judge LePage called the hearing to order. The family representative told of the condition he had found the house in. The handkerchief was introduced and identified by my friend's father. Except for our expressions, which must have been giveaways, there was the only real evidence against us—the bandanna and its laundry mark—but we weren't by nature liars and, our throats choked, fessed up with little nods to the big questions.

The case was dismissed with a lecture, a light sentence you might call it unless you'd been there. Judge LePage's words would have blistered asbestos.

The men filed out, offish and looking defiled by exposure to us, and by silent groups and singles started on their separate ways. I edged out alone, not wanting company, even that of my friend, and took a cross street and looked away yonder to the high hills which appeared cold but neutral. I knew I'd get more hell when I got home, cold but not neutral.

It was then I felt a hand on my shoulder. A voice said, "It's all over, Jase." A turn of my head, and I saw the friendly, little-smiling face of Chick Charleston, the sheriff who had found us out. His soft voice went on, "I know, Jase. It's almighty hard to be a kid."

So there was the beginning of friendship and trust. There was the beginning of my hanging around him and his office. And there was the reason for the white-chip position I occupied.

In the years right after my great disgrace, I grew up fairly tall, six feet plus a fraction. I had, I discovered, a strong right arm. I became a schoolboy pitcher and was good enough, though still in school, in time to pitch for the scrounged-up town team. As I got better I began to get paid, as much as ten dollars for some games. That money, plus sheriff's-office cash, was enough for me. Why bale hay or build fence or nurse stock in those long summer days? Besides, I would be in the big leagues before long. All I needed was better control. Which was why I squeezed a baseball—to strengthen my hand.

I never made the big time. I never tried to. I went to college instead and had a go, not brilliant, at creative writing. My teacher, a shriveled professor, complained I was prone to lapse into the lingo of the country in which I grew up.

No, the big leagues weren't for me. Though my right hand knit well enough, it still wasn't good enough, not after I broke it trying to save the life of Chick Charleston.

CHAPTER THREE

"You savvy much about firearms, Jase?" the sheriff asked me.

It was morning of the same day I had returned from my joy ride in the old hearse. I had got out of bed early, choosing to miss sleep rather than goings-on, and had had breakfast and come right to the office. There had been few people about, and none knew enough to be curious yet.

"Nothing much," I answered. "I own a twenty-two pump and a shotgun, half-choke, both of them Winchesters."

Charleston was fingering a couple of cartridges, one for a revolver, I guessed, and one for a rifle, their calibers not plain to me. "Buster Hogue's still alive, but that's all," he said. "Never a chirp from the poor bird." He studied the cartridges in his hand and added, "Funny."

I waited for him to explain, but he didn't speak for a while. He just sat there, half out from behind his desk, and his eyes went from the shells he held to the shiny toe of one boot, as if a clue might be scuffed on it.

Then he said, getting up, "Damn court would be in session today and need me as a witness in a pisswillie case. Ought to be through at noon. You want to take a ride with me at, say, about one o'clock?"

I told him I did but, before he could go, Old Doc

Yak came galloping in, satchel in hand, to treat a prisoner whose hangover woes could be heard now and then in the office. The man, taken drunk at a country bar, had shot at a friend, missed, and punctured a slop pail. Charleston waited for Doc to return from the cells in back. "Paraldehyde," Doc said as he came out. "That'll gentle the snakes."

"Hold it, Doc," Charleston said.

"For what?"

"Buster Hogue."

"You know all I do. Serious wound."

"Yeah. How well was it treated?"

"Best of my ability."

"Sure. Sure. I mean before. By that Doctor Pierpont?"

"Adequate."

"No more than that?"

"What the hell? Adequate is adequate."

"And professional courtesy is professional courtesy?"

"Goddam it, Chick, he's a psychiatrist." Doc Yak snorted. "Mental healing for loose bowels. Anyhow, he's not accustomed to country sawbones work. Not his field. And what's the big idea, my friend?"

"Nothing, I guess."

"And I guess you're right." Doc grunted and thumped out.

I left the office then and looked up Terry Stephens, who had been laid off from unloading a couple of freight cars because the cars were unloaded. As a catcher he wasn't good enough for the team, but he was always willing to catch my practice pitches. On our way to the vacant lot alongside the Great Northern depot where there was a board fence for a backstop, we kept stopping to tell the curious the Buster Hogue score, or as much of it as we knew. And we held up long enough to watch and hear old Mrs. Jenkins, who was yelling out, "Let the lower lights be burning . . . ," while enroute to the post office. I figured her lights were burning pretty low.

I practiced and fooled around with Terry for a couple of hours, went home and studied my book on fingerprinting and had lunch with my mother and dad and told about last night's shooting. My dad, an abstracter, said with a semi-serious smile, "Chick and you will uncover the culprit. Chick alone if duty calls you elsewhere," meaning to the pitcher's mound. He didn't oppose my baseball ambition. He just treated it lightly.

The sheriff was waiting for me. He told old Jimmy to man the office and led out to his car, which was his own (not the county's) and brought him maybe enough money in mileage for operation and maintenance. It was a modified machine with plenty of clearance, unlike the factory jobs that high-centered on horse turds and cost punctured gas tanks and lost mufflers on country roads. It had extra-ply tires, a hand choke for cold-weather starting and power enough for the law's purposes. He called it his Rocky Mountain Special.

"Where to, Jase?" he asked, as if he hadn't already made up his mind.

"To the scene of the crime, I s'pose."

"We'll dude it first."

He meant we'd go see Guy Jamison, the dude rancher.

It was an agreeable enough drive. For seven miles we followed the new highway that wasn't quite super but was called that. It carried a lot of traffic—summer tourists, logging trucks and assorted vans bound to and from Canada. Then we turned off onto what Loose had called that rocky-assed road.

Bouncing around, seeing high summer on all sides and the blued mountains lifting clear in the sunshine, I felt good, good to be in this, my own climate and country, good to be with Charleston, good to know I was pitching come Sunday. I had brought the baseball along and gave it a squeeze or two when I remembered.

We found Guy Jamison in his toolshed working on packhorse rigging, I imagined in preparation for the big-game season. He laid aside the rigging and put down a ball-peen hammer as we pulled up and got out. He was lean and muscular, as a man had to be to heave and hitch packs on a pack string, and his eyes had the squint of the guide in them, the mountain squint that could see elk and bear where dudes couldn't. His smile made his face different from common sober.

"Time to talk awhile, Guy?" Charleston asked.

"Sure thing. Dudes are out riding, or fishing. Come on up to the house."

The house was his new lodge. We called out hello to his wife, who along with a cabin girl was hanging sheets on a line. Inside, we took seats in the lodge room, and Guy offered beer, which I refused, the higher law being present, and Charleston accepted.

"Some place you've got," the sheriff said, looking around, after Guy had come back with the bottles.

It was some place, as clean and joined and close-built as a cabinetmaker could ask.

"Thanks," Guy said like a man who couldn't take compliments easily. "If it ever pays off." He took a sip of beer. "What's the word on Buster Hogue?"

"Still alive but still out. Guy, were you on hand all during the picnic?"

"Mostly. I didn't have time to sneak off and shoot." Guy's smile transformed his face again.

"I mean, did you note anything, like absences from the group, that might be significant? Who was present around the fire, and who wasn't, when Buster got hit?"

"I can't help you, Chick. I had my dudes there and rode herd on them when I wasn't passing them grub from the chuck wagon I'd brought along as a sort of special attraction, as an extra treat, you might say."

"Quite a treat."

"Yeah. I thought maybe they'd jump the reservation, some of them, after the shooting, but, Jesus Christ, no! They've seen the wild west, just like in pictures, and can't be pried off the place until their set time runs out."

"Did you talk to Hogue at all?"

"For maybe one minute. He was riding his conservative horse, bitching about high taxes, government spending, government waste, humbuggery at all levels."

"Did you happen to see whether Hogue took off his hat?"

"What the hell? Oh, sure. Pretty bald. Pretty target. No. I didn't notice."

"Loose Lancaster said he did."

"And who except for the guilty party would have an eye for it? But Lancaster? That's loco, Chick."

"I suppose, but it's an interesting if unlikely item. Who notices when a man uncovers? Or who remembers without special reason?"

Guy got up to fetch more beer. The sheriff scuffed his chin with his knuckles, gave me a little grin and asked, "Any questions?"

I didn't have any, but I noticed that Charleston took off his hat on entering the room and so had a bit of evidence to offset his observations.

"All right, then," the sheriff said after Guy had returned with fresh bottles. "You didn't see anything that would stir up suspicion. You say Loose Lancaster is out. And now tell me, Guy, just who has had trouble with Hogue. All of them that you know."

Guy smiled that surprising smile and answered, "Who hasn't?" He fingered out a cigarette and lit it with a kitchen match. "You can start with me."

"Shall I?"

"You might. A motive you're after. Well, Hogue won't keep up his fences. He leaves my gates down. I've got just enough graze for my own horses, none to feed his damn cattle. We've had a run-in or two. Make it four at the least."

"So?"

"Make no mistake. I've got a temper. When I was greener, before I wised up, I told our friend Hogue I was dickering for a quarter section of land I needed for pasture. Next thing I knew, Hogue had bought it out from under me. When I braced him, he just smiled and said, 'Business is business.' We had it hot and heavy. I could have killed him."

For an instant Guy's face set itself in old rage. Then it relaxed. "A thing with me," he went on, "is I can't remain mad. Call it a weakness, but, anyhow and moreover, to stay mad is to eat your guts out. You have no time but for anger, none for the business at hand."

"Right," Charleston said, nodding.

"And in spite of all, believe it or not, I kind of like the old bastard. You can grade him blow-hard and loud-fart, sort of amusing itself, and he sure God has been greedy for land, but, if he'd diddle you one way or another and let his cows in on your grass, in time of real need he'd give you, well, not the shirt off his back, but his old one. Yep. More or less likable."

Charleston was turning his sand-colored hat in his hands. "We can cross off your dudes as witnesses, I would think. They wouldn't have seen anything."

"Except scenery, and it through bifocals or camera finders. Good bunch but city-bred blind."

"Then name me who's had trouble with Hogue."

Guy gave him a look that seemed to say Charleston ought to know a thing or two without asking and then answered, "Ben Day's number one."

"Outside of him, for the time being."

"I would say all whose land butts on his. Offhand, Oscar Oliphant, Blue Piatt, Loose Lancaster, Plenty Toogood, Taller-Ass McNair."

We were strong on nicknames, I better explain. Blue Piatt's initials were B. L. U., standing for what nobody knew. Plenty Toogood's first name was Robert but never used unless on a mortgage or check. Taller-Ass McNair was a real old old-timer who in days before mine kept his saddle anointed with mutton tallow, which put a brand on his britches.

"I've already talked to Loose, Oliphant and Piatt," the sheriff said. "No good as witnesses. As suspects?" He shrugged. "Well." For a long minute there was silence. Then he asked, "What about your hermit?"

"Chouquette." Guy gave it the local pronunciation, which was Shoo-cat. "Pierre wasn't there, of course, unless hiding out with a rifle. Once he butchered one of Hogue's steers, as a warning against trespass, I guess. Nothing much came of that except hot words and winter meat for Pierre."

"There's that newcomer, Professor Powell Hawthorne, isn't it? Doesn't his land abut Hogue's? Have you met him?"

"Yes to all questions. Met him and his daughter both—God, what a filly—last night at the picnic and just once before. The place—it's a full section, you know, with a nice cabin on it—was left to him by his brother. You remember old Spike Hawthorne? Gone most of the time, wintering in Phoenix, and died and was buried there six, eight months ago."

"I knew him to speak to."

"Buster tried to get hold of that section, I hear. The professor said no. He's a retired geologist, so they say, and will just summer there, studying rocks and the birds and the bees. I would call him an old-fashioned gentleman, ivy brand." Guy paused and then threw in, "He's quite a historian and collector, too. Got a nice lot of old guns."

"Old guns!"

"Sharps, Henrys, Colts and more. But hold up, Chick. I doubt he ever fired one. Trouble with Hogue? Not to my knowledge. It's your guess whether he saw anything at the picnic."

Charleston finished his beer and said no to another. I remembered I hadn't squeezed the baseball in some time and so began squeezing it.

"So we come to the doctor," the sheriff said.

"Ulysses Pierpont. How's that for a monicker? Goes nice with psychiatrist. You met him?"

"Not even seen him."

"He's new this summer and comes up from the city just when his practice allows. He picked up a few acres, just a patch, at a tax sale none of us noticed at the time. Got a small trailer house on it but big plans for the future. That's the word, anyhow. Me, I saw him for the first time last night."

"To talk to?"

"Not much. A little, after Buster was shot. I just thanked the Lord he was there. He knew his business."

"So Doc Yak told me. But for him, he said, Buster would have died on the way in to town."

"Yeah. Pierpont didn't say so, but I guess he thought the case was hopeless regardless. I know he looked grave and was shaking his head when we carried Hogue off."

"No bad blood between them?"

"Nuts, Chick."

"And no prior contact?"

"None I could swear to. I did hear, true or false, that Doctor Pierpont wanted to buy a quarter section from Hogue to add to his patch, but he wanted to get hold of the Hawthorne place, too. No soap either time. That don't make a case for you, for God's sake."

Charleston ran a hand over his head, started to say something and didn't, and asked after a while, "What about threats to Hogue, from the men mentioned already?"

"For what they're worth. Blue Piatt said he'd kill Hogue if he didn't keep his cows inside his own fences. That's for sure. I heard it. One of Hogue's boys, little Buster, it was, said in my presence that Oscar Oliphant had shoved him and a bunch of strayed beef off his place with a rifle. Loose Lancaster runs off at the mouth, and so what? Pierre Chouquette, well, he did butcher a steer, but, besides that, who knows what goes on in the mind of that Indian hermit? You can forget old McNair. He's a friend and more or less a retainer of Hogue's."

Guy lighted another cigarette, inhaled and studied Charleston through the smoke he breathed out. "Why dodge Ben Day?"

The sheriff smiled a thinking smile, which uncovered teeth a girl would have prized, her jaws allowing. It was when he smiled that you realized how clear blue his eyes were. There was good nature in his face, good nature mixed with fixed purpose; and it struck me as I looked at him that I wouldn't want to be the man he was after but, having been caught, would be glad he was the man who had caught me.

"I know," he said. "Any fool would point first to Day."

"Why not? He had the biggest trouble with Buster."

"So I've heard. But that was smoothed over, you know, and never got to my office. What's your version?"

"Hearsay, same as yours. Day had a Forest Service

permit and damn few cows to trail up to mountain pasture. His count was about two hundred short of his allowance. That's what they say. So he made a deal with Buster by which Buster would use that summer graze."

Charleston shrugged and said just as a side remark, "And to hell with regulations."

"Sure. Neither one cared about government rules. But to play safe from nosy rangers, they changed the brands on those cattle, from Buster's to Day's. About then Day had a bright idea, or maybe he had had it before. On the strength of the brand he mortgaged the cattle."

As if to a story heard before, the sheriff nodded. "And got found out."

"Somehow. I don't know the straight of it. Seems Buster got his cattle back and the bank—the Second State in the city, I heard—the bank recovered its loan, and that was that. Never a charge made."

"Because Buster couldn't come into court with clean hands."

"And banks don't like stinks, long as the cash drawer isn't short."

"A big hush-hush all around," Charleston said, and blew out a deep breath. "No little birds telling me how Buster and Day feel now, one toward the other."

There was a question in his words, and Guy answered, "Me, neither. But it stands to reason they're not what you would call bosom pals. Not Mr. Ben Day, anyhow."

The sheriff got up and said, "All right, Guy. Thanks. Come on, Jase."

As we stood there about to go, Mrs. Jamison and the cabin girl came in, looking a little flushed from the sun. We said a few things back and forth, but what I noticed was the eye that cute cabin girl had for the sheriff. Good God, she was too young and fresh for him. He must have been forty and a long ways from fresh.

While we were on the way to the car, Guy called out, "How's the old wing, Jase?" as if to make up for leaving me out of the conversation.

"Felt good this morning," I called back, waving the

baseball, and Charleston and I climbed into the Rocky Mountain Special.

Once we were on the way, Charleston said, "Now we'll dodge in on the picnic grounds."

We pulled up on the ridge overlooking the bottom. The ridge had a few stunted pines on it and some creeping juniper and, in the gravel and dry grass, a crisscross of tire tracks left by the cars that had parked there.

The bottom was a sweet place, open except for the willows flanking the river, which here made a bend and had gouged out a trout hole as deep and blue as a fisherman's dream. At the east end of the little flat stood Jamison's canvas-clad chuck wagon, which could have been gotten down the steep, bouldered slope only by Jamison's high-wheeled, four-wheel-drive truck. In the center was the dead picnic fire. From above, it was the only sign of last night's get-together, except for half a dozen wooden blocks sawn for seats. Even with a shooting to draw top attention, someone or more had remembered to pick up the trash.

We scrambled down the ridge and went to the remains of the fire. One of the blocks had been overturned and lay on its side. Studying it and the ground close around, Charleston pointed to a small patch of gravel and grass, stained and coated with what I knew wasn't rust. He began taking sightings, moving a little this way and that while his eyes reconnoitered the ridge. He wasn't saying anything, though, and I wandered off to the trout hole.

And almost the first thing I saw was a native trout like none seen before. Deep through the rippled water it shimmered, dark-backed, silver-sided, the five or six pounds of it holding upstream against the current with the barest pulse of its tail. Even before Charleston called, I knew I would have to come back with a fly rod, and I slid away so as not to alarm it.

Back on the crest of the ridge, Charleston moved from one place to another, his eyes on the ground. I didn't know what he looked for until he said, "Jase, it's damn unlikely it was any kind of automatic, which would eject the casing itself, but isn't it likely that a man used to guns would work the lever or pump without thinking? Unless, of course, he'd thought about that."

We scuffed through the grass and examined the gravel without results, and then got back in the car.

"Now," the sheriff told me when we were rolling again, "we'll drop in to pass the time of day with Mr. Ben Day."

I spoke the thought that came to me. "Mr. Charleston, excuse me, but oughtn't you to be armed?"

He turned long enough to grin at me and answer, "My cause is just."

I wasn't wise enough then to hook up his words to the quotation.

We drove on toward Ben Day's, some five or six miles farther down. The sky was deep and blue any way you looked, and the wind as quiet as the sun in the grass. It would have been a good day for baseball, and it was hard to think that anyone hereabouts, on this summer-kissed afternoon, could have taken a pot shot at Buster.

Day's place was just a so-so ranch with plenty of acreage but most of it stony and pretty bald. In sight after we turned into the half-mile dirt lane came the sprawl of house and weather-battered outbuildings and quite a lot of machinery, some of it broken and discarded and the remainder neglected, all standing or lying in faded red and green colors. A couple of orphaned lambs—we called them bums—bawled for handouts at the back door, though they were big enough to rustle for themselves. A gopher flirted his tail at the edge of a scattered woodpile. We had no more than pulled up when Day opened the back door and came out. We left the car and went to meet him, Charleston, of course, in the lead.

"Hello," Charleston said. "Nice afternoon."

Day looked friendly. He always looked friendly. He had a toothpick in his mouth and tongued it to one side so's to answer. "Howdy, Sheriff. Always glad to see you."

You wouldn't think a man could make a toothpick insulting, not with a grin to go along with it.

"Good," Charleston said. "You know why I'm here."

"Let me take a guess. You wouldn't be hawkshawin' around?"

"Just asking questions."

"And Ben Day, he's your man. Sorry, Sheriff, I don't know a damn thing, except the radio just said old Hogue was still hangin' on."

"Yeah. I'm trying to locate any party or parties that saw anything at the picnic."

"Wrong number."

"Or did anything?"

"Guilty, Your Honor. I et, thinkin' that was what to do at a picnic."

While the sheriff sized him up, he stood slouching easy in his work clothes—denim shirt, denim pants hitched low and corral-stained, western hat cocky-cocked on his head. Wind and fists had coarsened his face. His nose slanted off from an old break.

"Cut it out!" The sheriff's voice had an edge to it now. "You didn't see anything or do anything, so you say. Were you with the bunch all the time?"

"I be goddamned." Day's tone was still soft. "Does a man have to have a permit to piss? Maybe I did piss, goin' off by myself on account, you know, of ladies bein' present. Maybe I climbed the hill to my pickup for a bottle or more cigarettes. Maybe."

"Maybe you did. Maybe you saw, time of the shot, whether Buster had his hat on or off?"

"No help. The hat ought to tell you."

"Thanks."

The sheriff turned away. I was thinking of more questions to ask, though I didn't suppose they would have got answers, not from that mocking and insolent and confident ex-con.

Before we reached the car, Day called, "You're welcome. Just let me know if I can help."

We were near town before Charleston spoke again, and then all he said was, "One thing I would bet on. He climbed the ridge."

CHAPTER FOUR

Buster Hogue's condition remained the same the next day, which was Saturday. The hospital had him marked down as critical, no visitors, and a neurosurgeon had been called in on the case.

That's what the sheriff told me when I showed up bright and early. He was drinking a cup of coffee, the sheriff was, and old Jimmy was hovering around as if he thought Charleston should spring into action like a goosed frog. Jimmy was a good lockup man and got along fine with the prisoners, no doubt because he had been a live wire himself before age cut down on the current. Now and then he had a beer, saying he had drunk enough of the hard stuff to give the D.T.'s to all the hard cases on record. These were about the sum of his qualities, though. As a detective he rated somewhere around minus one.

Charleston wasn't springing, not yet. For all I could tell he was just fooling around in his head, his face relaxed and his eyes exploring his thoughts. He did say, "Saturday. Nobody home likely, unless old McNair or Chouquette."

I asked, "Anything for me?"

"Maybe later."

So I excused myself and walked down to old Mrs. Jenkins' house. It was a white, rambling picket-fenced place with a chicken run in the rear, all left to her by her late husband, who had died to the tune of "Bringing in the Sheaves," though he didn't hear it, having gone conveniently deaf some time before. That was the story around town, anyhow, but you had to allow for embroidery.

Once and sometimes twice a week Mrs. Jenkins wanted me to chop the head off a fryer so's to have meat in the skillet and no blood on her hands. Also to make sure she didn't cut off a finger while performing the execution herself.

She gave me good-morning after I had knocked on the door and said yes to the butchering and sailed back in the house, resting her vocal chords, I guessed, for the parade to the post office.

I caught and decapitated the chicken, collected the customary two bits and went away to the hummed blessing of "Work for the Night Is Coming."

Even with the almost-super highway skirting the town, the place was busy, not yet having accepted the idea that Saturday and Sunday were one in the realm of nongainful endeavor. It was Mabel Main's day off, though, and she came coursing down Main Street with the high-kneed gait of a harness horse. She was all bone and fast action, and she was also the best telephone operator ever known, which was why she had survived automation. When the company proposed to replace her with dials and wrong numbers, the subscribers threatened to cancel out and establish a co-op. So Mabel stayed on, being charged up to good will, it would seem. She knew everything. If Mrs. Smith gave her Mrs. Jones' number, she would say, that being the case, "This is Mrs. Jones' day to play bridge at Mrs. Sandusky's. Want me to ring her there?" The telephone office provided a good lookout, too. So Mabel knew when Frank Featherston was visiting Mrs. Younce, the widow, because she could see Frank's old faithful setter waiting on Mrs. Younce's porch for Frank to finish his business. That last bit is one of the truths or part-truths that a young fellow picks up, barely believing.

Mabel said to me, "Howdy, Deputy, you fireballer. How's the sleuth?"

"Sleuthing."

"And the high sheriff? Too busy, I bet, to pass the time of day, huh?"

There was a look on her face that seemed to say more than the words. Did she have something to tell him, something she'd listened in on? Or was it that she just hankered to see him, being more than a bit smitten, as people said? Eeny, meeny. I could see her going for him but not him for her, though at forty or thereabouts he couldn't hope for the pick of the field. Miny, mo.

"Leave it to him," I told her.

She let out a *humph* and left me, striding knees high.

Buster Junior was leaning against the front of the Bar Star Saloon. He was a muscular, mouthy and ill-tempered son of a bitch, and why he and Ben Day hadn't tangled I didn't know. One of those accidents of time and opportunity, probably. Or brother peas in a pod.

I asked about his father.

What he answered was, "That goddam sheriff! What's he doin'? Ironin' a crease in his britches on account of he sits down so much? Tell him to get off his ass."

I doubted that I could whip him, but still I could feel my pitching arm tense. And it worked against me that he was older by several years—which made a big psychological difference at age seventeen.

"You tell him," I said, "but I wouldn't advise it."

He was mouthing something as I turned and walked off.

Otto Dacey was coming up the street with his blank look and damp pants. He was the swamper, meaning sweeper, that I've told about, and wasn't allowed in the bar until closing time, which usually meant that the saloon closed on time. You couldn't get upwind from him there.

He stopped and shook his head sadly and said as I maneuvered away from his scent, "That poor Mrs. Jenkins."

"Yeah, Otto, but she gets along," I answered.

He kept shaking his head. "People crazy. So many."

I savvied his reference. Once he had been sent to the asylum—Central State Hospital we called it, being nice about stigma—and after a few months had been certified sane and released. It was his pride, his mark of superiority, that he was the one man in the county whose sanity had been tried, tested and proven. Sometimes I thought he was right, though he still peed his pants and, when he happened to think about it, peed in the gutter—which last was the reason he'd been sent to the asylum on a count of repeated indecent exposure.

I said, "We're all crazy but you, Otto," and walked away accompanied by his smile.

It was too early for lunch, and so I went to our backyard and practiced control, using an old door on which I'd sketched an exact home plate with some leftover paint. The strikes had a bare edge over balls.

To this day I don't know why Chick Charleston took me along on that summer's trips unless it was that company helped him parcel his thoughts out. Or unless it was that, like any man, he liked someone to ride with and chose the first convenient free soul. Anyway, we hadn't gone far that afternoon, bound for old Taller-Ass McNair's place, when he said, "That bullet, Jase, it ricocheted off Buster Hogue's skull. Hit it and veered up. What do you make of that?"

"Foul tip," I said.

"Oh, pisswillie. You keep shaking hands with that baseball, and pretty soon your head will be diamond-shaped. If it's not too much to ask, take your mind off your mitt and aim it at bone head and firepower."

He was smiling as he spoke, smiling that easy, disarming smile of his which suggested peace, not police, but still held the hint of purpose and force to go with it.

I said, "All right, Sheriff," and at once began thinking about next day's ball game, which was against Bear Paw and was sure to be tough, that team by report having recruited three or four city ringers.

But neither ball game nor shooting was enough to fill my mind by itself, not on a day like today with the air clear and clean as at the beginning of time, with the green-fringed, business-as-ever river to our left and the wild grasses barely saluting the breeze. It was a day for the final, elusive truth to come out of hiding.

McNair's place lay west of the Rose River—which meant we had to follow the highway, take Loose Lancaster's road for about twenty miles and then turn

left and cross the one bridge over the stream, passing
the picnic grounds on the way. Thereafter the road was
little more than an old wagon trail, flanked and cen-
tered with boulders that a driver had to snake through,
else lose his car's guts on the everlasting stone. And the
road that swung off of it to the coulee in which McNair
had his shack was even worse. Which was one reason
why federal agents hadn't closed down his still in the
old Prohibition days before mine. Another was, I'd
been told, that his moonshine was almost as good as
prescription whiskey, and what agent didn't like a good
drink when his day's work was done?

McNair's house was little more than a shed. There
was an old wagon beside it with one broken wheel and
a beat-up Ford that might have been bought from old
Henry himself. A pitcher pump stood rusty at one side
of the shack and a pile of saw logs at the other. They
were just about the total of exterior decoration except
for a little wash bench with a bucket on it and a rag of a
hand towel that drooped from a nail.

A big, surly dog ran from behind the house, charged
close and dared us to get out of the car. While I
hesitated, wishing for a ball bat, the sheriff dismounted.
He stooped and spoke and held out his hand. "Easy,
you potlicker," he said, his tone soft. The dog took a
sniff and retreated a yard or two, growling but undecided.

Old Man McNair appeared at the door, pulling his
hat down against the sun's glare. He waited, wordless.

I got out of the car, keeping an eye on the dog. I
never had been crazy about dogs, not since a neighbor's
pet bit me while I was stooped under a currant bush
trying to retrieve my baseball.

The sheriff said, "Howdy. Nice afternoon."

The old man had a beak that an eagle would have
accepted with thanks, sharp eyes set close beside it and
a mustache fertilized by tobacco. As a baby he must
have been rocked to sleep while astraddle a barrel. But,
for all his years and bowlegs, he looked fit enough.

"Goddam heel flies," he said to the sheriff's greeting. He spit at a wild showy daisy, turning it into a
sunflower.

"Ease off, old pardner," Charleston said. "Thought you'd want to know Buster Hogue's holding on."

"Thanks." The old cuss didn't mean thanks. He meant get the hell gone.

The sheriff studied him as if wondering where to use a pry bar. Then he asked suddenly, "You at the picnic?"

McNair let out, "Where else?" and spit again.

"So maybe you picked up some ideas?"

"Keep guessin'."

"Ideas like who did it?"

"Sons of bitches."

"That's for sure. Who?"

"Find out."

"I'll do just that," Charleston said. He added, "Given some help."

"I done sold out the last batch. Waitin' for a new order."

The sheriff took a bandanna—silk, it looked like— from a pocket of his creased pants and used it on his forehead. "Hot here in the sun," he said.

It was sure-enough hot. The sun burned down out of a sky that had never seen a cloud and never hoped to see one. In the distance you could see the earth breathing heat waves.

"Thirsty weather," Charleston told McNair. "You got a bucket inside, I suppose."

Without waiting for yes or no, he veered around the old man and started through the open door. McNair turned to follow, saying nothing. That left me and that ugly stud dog, who had lain growling at the side of the shack and now made a sashay to get at my heels, but I pulled my arm back, baseball in hand, and so fazed him long enough for a skip through the doorway.

Inside, there were a rickety stand table together with bucket and dipper, a straight chair held upright by baling wire, a wooden block to accommodate company, a bed with an old soogan on it, a sheet-metal stove with firewood beside it and an up-ended apple box decorated with a tin plate and one fork, both unwashed. They were about all I took in at first glance. Then I saw that

Charleston had stopped before a deer-antler rack nailed to the wall. The horns cradled an old rifle, and one prong served as a hook for a hat. McNair had curved by him and was about to plant his old butt on the bed.

"Spanish-American War?" Charleston said. I guessed his reference was to the rifle.

McNair answered, "One kind. Springfield forty-five seventy. Hands off."

"Wasn't about to," Charleston told him. He moved over and took a drink from the dipper and let himself down on the block. Seeing that McNair had taken the bed now, I perched myself on the chair.

"You're Buster's friend?" Charleston asked.

"Heel flies and sons of bitches." The old man spit the words out.

The sheriff paid no mind. "Now you take Blue Piatt or Oscar Oliphant or Pierre Chouquette or even Loose Lancaster—they aren't what you could call Buster's friends." The sheriff had spoken softly, as if just reviewing the prospects in his own mind.

"Ask 'em."

"Uh-huh." Now the sheriff leaned forward, and his eyes bored at McNair. "How about Ben Day?"

"I never seen nothin'. I don't say nothin'. Quit your goddam buzzin'."

"Not yet, old-timer. You know as well as anybody that Ben and Buster had trouble, but Buster couldn't push charges because he himself was outside the law. Ben held a grudge, though. I'll lay odds."

"Damn your heel-fly soul! You shut up about Buster! Best man in the country, and shot down now, and you blackenin' his good name."

The sheriff gave the old man a long, unmoving study. Then he said, "A friend, you call yourself," and again fell silent. After the pause he pointed abruptly toward the horn rack, and even before he spoke I suspected it wasn't the rifle alone that he had been looking at. "That hat there. Seems to have a hole in it. Or holes."

From where I sat all I could see was that the hat

was an old one, once probably off-white and still pretty pale.

"I declare," the old man answered, calm as could be and as insolent. "Could have been tromped on by a calk-shod horse, a bronc."

"Whose hat?"

McNair pushed his own hat back on his head and to my surprise answered, "Buster Hogue's."

"So?"

"Damn picnic fools left it, totin' Buster away. I picked it up. That's how come."

Charleston got up, went over and examined the hat and said, "Hm-m." Then he put it back on the prong and turned to McNair. "Lancaster said he had taken his hat off, and so his bald head served fine as a target."

"His name is Loose."

"Nickname." The sheriff motioned to me, and I came to my feet and went out with him.

The dog growled us into the Special.

We were quiet while Charleston wound the car over the bouldered trail, but when the going got easier I asked the little question that was first in my mind. "What's this heel-fly business, Sheriff? Heel flies, he kept saying."

"Old name," Charleston told me. "Some time, way back, the law was after him. Heel flies, that was what rustlers and cowpunchers on the run called sheriffs and deputy marshals."

I could understand, having seen livestock on the bolt from the pests. "It says it," I said.

"Better than fuzz." The sheriff turned left on the main trail, away from the town. "McNair's set against the likes of us two. Whatever he saw and whatever he knows, he'd play tight-mouth with the law. Guilty or not guilty, witness or no."

I made bold to ask, "And the hat?"

"Hard telling," he answered, "but it wasn't calks made those holes."

I didn't press him, but it seemed to me that the hat, being pale, would have served as a target almost as

well as Buster's bald head. Almost, but not quite,
which maybe was the reason that Buster still lived. But,
saying the hat was the mark, what happened to Loose's
story that Buster had taken it off? And where did it
leave Loose?

Pretty soon I realized we were bound for Pierre
Chouquette's. The place lay in the scrub pine in a gulch
close to the river. I knew it from fooling around while
out fishing.

Charleston pulled up a few yards from the cabin,
which looked old-maid tidy, something you wouldn't
expect from a hermit. Beyond it was a little barn and a
store of corral poles set on their butts against the
weather and sloped in to the top, tepee fashion. They
were one of Chouquette's sources of income. Beyond
the barn the gulch opened up into wide, slanting fields
that rose to a butte.

"Nobody home," I said.

"Sure?"

"The running gear to his lumber wagon is gone,
and so are those two old horses of his. They'd be in the
catch pasture this time of year or in the shade of the
barn. Likely he's gone into the canyon for logs or more
poles."

To make certain, Charleston gave a couple of blasts
with his horn and, getting no answer, settled back in his
seat.

Here, beside the little cabin, we might have been
alone in the world. There was a sort of free desolation
about the place, as if the owner had been taken away
and left as proof of his once being only the forsaken
work of his hands. There came to my mind, while the
silence sang around us, a couple of lines liked by my
father. "They are all gone away. There is nothing more
to say." The sight and clucks of a brood of blue grouse—I
counted six plus the mother hen—pointed up the absence
of man, whom the earth had been made for but wasn't
his anymore.

The sheriff's voice brought me up with a bump.
"Jase," he said, and got out one of the two or three thin
cigars he rationed himself day by day. After he had it

going, he went on, "The fix we're in reminds me of old Chet Bayliss."

"Bayliss?"

"Down south. You wouldn't know him. He lived by himself, Chet did, in a cabin—a house it was really— ten, twelve miles from town. He had enough to get along on, having saved up his money just so, in old age, he could get away and not be pestered by people. Toward the human race he was like our friend, Chouquette, here. Four miles away a lawyer, name of Bill Rogers, had a summer and weekend cabin. They got to be good friends, strange to say."

The sheriff drew deep on his cigar and breathed out the smoke slow, seeing that other time and organizing his story.

"Trouble had come to Chet earlier. It was his eyes. Cataracts. But he had them operated on and could see all right, all right as long as he wore specs as thick as ice cubes. Without them he couldn't be sure about daylight and dark. So he had them on his nose all the time, except when he went to bed he laid them on a little table close to his head. You savvy?"

I said I did, and the sheriff breathed out another slow puff.

"We go back to Bill Rogers, the lawyer. His trouble was pack rats. You have to keep after those varmints or they'll chew up the place and get in the house one way or another, even down a stovepipe and out through the damper, and they'll gnaw what can be gnawed and what can't and leave trails of such shit as would embarrass a hog."

"That's what I've heard," I said, and thought to squeeze my neglected baseball.

"Bill got after them. Not with poison, for that killed off the chipmunks and squirrels, but with traps. He bought half a dozen and set them in old lengths of stovepipe, laid flat, which rats like to travel, and he placed a couple of them behind a wornout door put on its side and angled against the wall of his barn."

Charleston looked at his cigar and decided on a drag or two more before going on.

"Came the day. Saturday and just sunup, it was, and Bill Rogers hustled from town to run his trap line. First off, he looked at the barn door. One chain was tight, so he knew he had a catch there under cover. He hunted up a stick to knock the rat in the head with.

"Stick in hand, he swung back the door, and, by God, he had a catch all right, but it was a skunk and, what's more, ass-aimed right at him. It let fly.

"Bill dropped the door back and gave himself two seconds for shock and two more for inspiration. He was that kind of a man."

The sheriff paused, for effect I supposed, but I couldn't help prodding him. "Then?" I asked.

"Then," he answered after more pause, "he walked to his car, got in and drove to Chet Bayliss' place. He was pretty sure Chet would still be in bed, him liking to sleep late, and he hid his car behind a bunch of aspen, went to the house and let himself in, slow and quiet. He tiptoed to Chet's bedroom. There he just stood. And stood and stood.

"And all at once Chet came out of his sleep, flicked open his poor eyes, took a trial sample of the air, snorted it out and clawed for his glasses. Before he could find them and get them set on his beak, Bill tiptoed out."

Abruptly, the tale told, Charleston put the cigar in his teeth, started the car and backed up for a turn-around. I was laughing.

"Last I heard," Charleston said after he had shifted gears, "old Chet was still talking about that goddam invisible skunk. Where it came from, how it got in and out, leaving no sign of itself except stink. Old Chet, never knowing the right of it."

We were back on the road to town now, and the sheriff concluded, "What? Who? Why? Whence and wherefore? The invisible skunk. There we are, Jase."

CHAPTER FIVE

We were the visiting team, and so most of the fans were against us, but we won the ball game, 5 to 3, and I went the route, though without much to brag about at the finish. For the record, just one of Bear Paw's three runs was earned, but no doubt about it. In the first inning one of the city ringers opposing us got the fat of his bat on a damn gopher ball and hit it about three cow pastures beyond my left fielder.

We kept pecking away, though, and at the bottom of the ninth, with only three outs to go, led by four runs. The first two men to come up we disposed of by a couple of miracles. Terry Stephens was catching, in the absence of our regular man who worked at Brick's Butcher and Locker Shop and had had to slaughter a steer, Sunday being no excuse for a let-up in blood-letting. The first batter fouled a ball that would have sailed over the back screen if there'd been one, or into the press box of a big-city park. Terry charged back for it, trampling a couple of kids and a dog in his chase but somehow keeping his feet. At the last minute, falling, he speared it. The second man up socked a line drive that our center fielder couldn't have caught in a month of Sundays, but this Sunday must have been one over the count, for he hauled the drive in over his shoulder.

Only one out to go, and some of the spectators were drifting away. So I walked the next man on four pitches. The next scratched a single. The next got on base when our shortstop fumbled his grounder. Bases loaded, then, and the tying run at the plate. The fans decided they were leaving too soon. They were.

Wild as a blind gunner, I walked in a run. I hit the next batter, and a second man scored. And at bat was that comedian who had murdered a pitch in the first inning.

Our manager—Felix Underwood, the undertaker— lagged out on the field to ask if I thought I should be embalmed, there being a live replacement of sorts. The dying man said he felt fine and was left to his fate.

I worked the count, or the comedian worked the count, to three and two. Terry Stephens came out to the mound. He said, "You're all right, Jase," and scuffed the ground, stalling for time. "You'll get him, the bastard. Blaze one through."

"Sure. Sure, Terry. Some foul catch you made."

Back of the plate again, Terry signaled for a fast ball, knowing I had better control with it than with a curve. But that joker at the plate was expecting a hard one, I felt sure, so I shook the sign off and fed the joker a curve that just caught the corner of the plate and left him looking. That was it, naturally, though the umpire got some hell for his call.

I knew why I lost control there in the ninth, though I wouldn't have confessed under torture. To get the picture, as they say, you must understand that those country-town ball parks had no grandstands or bleachers, only a couple of benches for players. People sat on the ground or stood up, back of the lines from home to first base and from home to third, and some of them watched from back of the catcher, to the rear of the postage-stamp backstop behind him, where they could make sure whether the umpire was blind. Drivers parked their cars beyond the sitters and standers, and a lot of the occupants looked on without getting out.

Of the two I saw him first, there at the end of the eighth inning. He was a trim, older man who wore a necktie, glasses and a Vandyke beard and appeared too bookish for baseball, but you never knew. In our region the national game was hanging on long after it had been reduced elsewhere to Little Leaguers and Babe Ruthers or whatever they called those tadpole teams. We had town teams, supported by townspeople, and the local loyalties were fierce. But whatever side he was on, I

figured the old gentleman—that was the word for him—
had come from his car to be in at the finish.

Then I saw the girl who moved up to his side, or,
rather, she burst on my sight. If there were better
words than freshness and loveliness, I would use them
to describe her. She was like a rare flower, sprung up by
magic from the weed patch. The lines of an old trail
song, sung by Terry to the soft strumming of his guitar,
ran in my head.

> *Eyes like the morning star,*
> *Cheeks like the rose . . .*

It was for her that I performed in that ninth inning.
It was because of her that I performed poorly. Self-
display goeth before bases on balls.

Bear Paw lay, and still lies, thirty miles from my
old hometown, all of them via the new highway except
for the turnouts into the two settlements. In spite of the
traffic, which was pretty heavy because of the tourists
and a just-ended rodeo farther up the line, we made
pretty good time. Five of us were in Terry's car, owned
by his old man, and five in Felix Underwood's, which
tailed us on the way home. Ten players were all we
could muster that day.

The entrances and exits into my town—which were
two in number and, for lack of overpasses or underpasses,
were both open to either exit or entry—were separated
by a half-mile or less. We had decided on the second
and lower road because it ran next to Hamm's Big
Hamburger stand.

But we hadn't gone far past the first turnout when
traffic slowed and came to a standstill, coming and
going. A lot of adventurers, balked in their pursuits of
paved distance, were leaning on their horns. Their
combined blasts would have satisfied the deafest of
rock-music hounds. And ahead, we could barely see, a
bunch of people, afoot, had gathered around something
we couldn't see. "Accident," Terry said.

We piled out of the car, my officer's duty running

high even in a baseball suit. The others followed me as we pushed through the gathering crowd to the march music of honks.

There, smack in one lane, lay a horse in harness and behind it a buggy. They blocked one lane. Curiosity blocked the other.

Then I saw Chick Charleston bending over the horse and an old codger bent over him. It took me a second to recognize Plenty Toogood.

Charleston gave an abrupt "Good!" to my "Hi, Sheriff."

Before he could go on, Toogood broke in. "Old Rex ain't dead, goddam your eyes!"

Felix Underwood, who ought to know, had pushed up for a look and a feel. He stood up to report, "Not yet."

Charleston nodded to the diagnosis, straightened and turned to Terry and me. "Terry," he said, "get the boys out. Post them at the turnouts. Have them flag down the drivers and route them through town."

"What with?" Terry asked.

"Your hats are red. So are your socks. Fix them on your bats."

"Right."

"And, Terry, when they can, have the stalled cars back up and take the detour. And for Christ's sweet sake and old Rex's, tell those horn players it's intermission."

Terry went away, and Charleston told me, "You, Jase, see if you can chase up Old Doc Yak."

Running, I wondered what Doc Yak could do. He wasn't above treating a horse, or a dog for that matter, since we had no resident vet, but how minister to an old bag-of-bones pelter that had decided to lie down and die?

Doc Yak wasn't home. He wasn't at his office. Then I saw his wreck of a car parked in front of the Bar Star Saloon. He wasn't one of those storybook, boozy medical men, but on occasion he was known to add a quick shot to his own store of restoratives.

I hurried him out of the place or would have done

so if necessary. You couldn't hurry Doc because he was always in a hurry himself. He put his car into first gear first, which was like him, and climbed the curb before he knew which way he was going. He should have been careful backing out, for the traffic from the highway had begun rolling through.

When we had got as close to the scene as we could, Doc grabbed his bag and hopped out, leaving his car to roll to a stand in Duke Appleby's yard. Duke got his lawn mower out of the way just in time, seemed about to yell something, then saw who the driver was and just smiled,

The situation was changing. There were the down horse and the buggy and Charleston, Toogood, Underwood and a few of the curious standing by, but the cars had thinned out, and the drivers weren't honking as if honks could waft away a dead horse. Terry and the boys were doing their job.

Doc didn't speak as he forged ahead to the patient. Anyone could see the horse was still breathing. Doc thumbed one of its eyelids and then forced its jaws open. He stood up to ask, "Just how goddam old is this animal?"

Plenty answered, "Not as old as you by a damn sight."

We were interrupted by a new arrival, a state patrolman, who said, "Hi, Chick," to Charleston. "What's the hitch?"

His arrival prodded Plenty into an explanation that I guessed he'd made earlier and often. "It was one of your men, damn your eyes," he told the patrolman. "That's the hitch. Just last week your pretty-prim joy boy said I couldn't see good enough to drive my car anymore. Said hell to pay if I did."

The patrolman said, "Yes?"

"Well, by God, old Rex sees good enough. Give him an eye test. Try arrestin' him, will you?"

The patrolman looked funny.

"So what do I do, havin' my car took out from under me, so to speak? I hitched up old Rex to that buggy there. Ain't been used for a coon's age, but it's solider than General Motors or Ford, you can bet your ass. Then I hit out for town. Would have made it, too, wasn't for these hell-crazy drivers, tearin' by, honkin' or draggin' ass to watch, like as if a horse and buggy had no right to the road. Damn their eyes!"

"What was the hurry? I mean, the purpose?"

"Hurry? Christ save me. To get to town. What else?"

While they had been talking, a sort of biography ran through my mind. Old Plenty Toogood had a place south of McNair's. It was a little haywire ranch held together by the squaw he said he was married to. Milk cow, chickens, a few hogs, maybe thirty beef cattle, all mostly tended by her. He said he was too old for hard work and, for that matter, probably was. But he wasn't too old for a drink or a dozen, which I guessed was what he was coming to town for.

Now he said, though we already saw, "See! I told you."

The horse had climbed to its feet. It stood drooping, ribs and hip bones showing and its ancient muscles a little atremble, but it stood.

"Nothin' the matter with him," Plenty told us.

"Except exhaustion," Doc Yak put in.

Charleston added, "And shock."

"Goddam right," Plenty said as if struck by a fresh idea. "Shock. These run-for-Jesus highways shock the shit out of better men than old Rex."

"Can he make it to the courthouse, taking it easy?" Charleston asked.

"Why not?"

"Get along then. I'll see you there," Charleston said. "We'll make arrangements to get you and your outfit back to the ranch. Not tonight. I'll find a place for the horse, and you can put up at the jail."

"Jail! And slam the bars, huh? All on account of a innocent horse."

"Naw. Naw," the sheriff said. "Just friendly accommodations. Get along."

Toogood climbed into the buggy, the like of which couldn't be seen except in museums, and slapped the old horse with the reins while he clucked to it. The

horse moved, bowed by the weight of centuries like the
man with the hoe.

Doc Yak picked up his bag. Felix Underwood
started back toward his car. The patrolman smiled
before leaving. "No charge," he said to Charleston.

"Unless cruelty to old animals, including old
Toogood."

When they had all gone, Charleston turned to me.
"Soon as Ben Hur turns into town, you can disperse
your posse, Jase. Tell the boys I'll set up the hamburg-
ers. Meet you there."

Walking away, I was struck with the thought that,
some way, among our lists of suspects for Buster Hogue's
shooting, Plenty Toogood had been lost in the shuffle.
We had mentioned his name only a time or two and
never asked him a question. I hadn't gone far, though,
until Charleston called, "Make it one down, Jase."

It took me a minute to figure that out.

CHAPTER SIX

There was no work for me the next day, or none to
speak of. Again I appeared at the office in good time,
thinking perhaps we'd drive out for more interviews,
but the sheriff had a more pressing engagement than
that of corralling a sniper.

"County commissioners are meeting today," he
said after reporting that Buster Hogue was still alive
but still blotto. He shuffled papers under his hand on
the desk. "Reports, bills, authorizations, all that stuff.
Pisswillie. And though it's none of their business, they'll
be curious about our crime wave. Damn curious."

"Especially Reverend Hauser," I said. The reverend had been elected because the pulpit made him an

honest man. My family being medium religious, I had been exposed to his on-high hellfire more than once. I went on to ask Charleston, "You ever hear him preach?"

Charleston gave me his smile, which sometimes but not now said more than his words. "I never heard him do anything else," he answered. "Why don't you go fishing, Jase? Wish I could."

I didn't go right away because a start at that hour would have put me on the river in the heat of the day, an unlikely time to catch trout. I hung around after he'd left and fooled around with my mail-order fingerprinting set which, the advertisement had indicated, would transform a simpleton into a sleuth. I hadn't brought my baseball along because my arm was sore from wild pitches.

In the jail was a roustabout, arrested for assaulting his wife, failure to support six snotty kids and other assorted charges, all of which could be proved to nobody's benefit. Jimmy Conner told me the man wanted to see me.

He was one of those men, born a nothing, who had spent his life proving he could be less than that. A harsh judgment but my own at the time. Even so, I could feel sorry for him.

"Hi, Claude," I said through the bars.

"You want to do me a favor, kid?"

"Depends," I answered. His eyes, streaked with red, and his face, swollen and painted by whiskey, suggested he wanted the drink I couldn't bring him.

"That goddam Buster Hogue!" he said. "If there was any man in him, he'd bail me out."

"From the hospital?"

"You know what he did? He gave me my time, that's what. No reason a-tall. Just hustled me to town and dumped me off and shorted me to boot on my pay."

"When?"

"When? How do I know when? I got drunk. Wouldn't you, bein' treated so mean?"

Jimmy Conner had come up to listen.

"Before Thursday? Before the annual picnic?"

"I guess so. Ask somebody."

"Who locked you up?"

Jimmy said, "I did. Off duty, too."

"What day, Jimmy?"

"Aw, the time fits, Jase, but nothin' else does. It was late Thursday night. No. Way early Friday morning, his missus called me. He ain't no culprit, not of the shootin'. You think Chick wouldn't have got on to him if he was?"

Charleston would have, of course. Any fool would have known that much.

Claude was saying, "About that favor, kid?"

What he wanted was an ad in the paper, thanking his friends for their kindnesses while he was behind the bars and, more than that, suggesting earnestly that he would appreciate further expressions of sympathy.

I asked him, "Who pays?"

"Boy," he answered, after searching the pockets he knew were empty, "it only costs two bits or so, and I figure I can trust you just like you can trust me."

In the office I wrote out a little ad, being weakened by his reasoning, and showed it to Jimmy.

Jimmy grinned in approval. "You know, his wife, bunged up as she was, brought him sandwiches and a cake, damned if she didn't. And two pals twice come in with a half-pint. I passed 'em on. What the hell, Jase? The law don't believe in cruel and unusual punishment. Now he's thirsty again and wants a repeat."

I took the ad to the *Clarion* and paid for it. It cost thirty-five cents.

Afterward, I picked up grub at the Commercial Cafe for Jimmy's two guests, delivered it and went home for lunch. My father said I could have the car, as long as it was fish and not fowl I meant to pursue. By "fowl" he meant pullets, which was another name he used for my dates.

All the time, driving, I kept thinking of that oversize trout, that wowser, that I had seen in the big hole alongside the picnic grounds. But I wouldn't start there. I would drive above it and fish downstream, hitting the hole along about sunset. There was good fishing on the way to it, in the neighborhood of the gully that hid Pierre Chouquette's place.

It was another one of those days, bright as new
brass, with not a cloud anywhere. It was hot enough for
you, as people ask in their sweat, lacking anything else
on their minds, but it would cool off later on, and a man
would feel released from midday embrace. I always thought
of late afternoon as kitten-fur soft. In the Northwest we
have days like that, day after summer day of burning sun
and hot breeze, and grain farmers look at the sky, fearing
hail. Then come the late-afternoon cool and the hours of
no-breeze, and all is right in the world.

The sun was relenting when I pulled off the road and
rigged my tackle. Until later, I figured, a wet fly, rather
large, would work better than a dry midget, and so I tied
to my leader a Size 8 Royal Coachman, that old reliable.

From the beginning the fishing was good, if not
extraordinary. By the time I came opposite Pierre
Chouquette's gulch, I had ten trout in my creel, all good
size for the pan. Some of them were cutthroats, the best
eating, and some rainbows, the gamest. Together they
made a good mess, as my old man would have said. I
decided then that I'd walk up the gulch and, on my own,
talk to Pierre, provided he had returned. So I shortened
my line and fixed the hook to the cork of the rod's butt
and set out on that quarter-mile stroll.

Before I saw Pierre, I knew he was home, for his
old team stood in the shade of the barn, fighting flies,
and his lumber wagon was pulled up in the yard. I
found Pierre behind his single-room residence, barking
a log with a draw knife. Someone must have ordered
peeled logs for a cabin.

He heard me before I told him hello and looked up
and smiled. He was a small man and polite, though a
hermit. Half French and half Cree or Chippewa, he had
a complexion tinted like a Brown Leghorn egg. He
hung his draw knife on a crotch of his sawbuck and
waited for conversation.

"Hard work," I said.

He made a little outward gesture of his hands, as if
I had exaggerated, and cast a glance to the west. "Stop
pretty soon," he answered.

"Don't let me interfere."

He said, "Weather, it will."

I looked to the west, too, and couldn't see a cloud, but I knew better than to challenge a man whose partner was nature. A mother blue grouse walked close to us, clucking to her unruly brood like a schoolteacher.

"Guess you've heard," I told him, "that there's some hope for Buster Hogue."

He answered, "Hogue?" not with like or dislike or a show even of interest.

"He's unconscious yet, but the bullet didn't go through his skull."

"So" was all I got out of him.

"You've heard about the picnic and him getting shot in the head by somebody unknown?"

"I go to the mountains for logs. But shot he was, you say. No doubt."

"In his bald spot, by the light of the moon. The sheriff's hot on the trail of whoever did it."

"Many people do not like Buster Hogue."

"Including you, Pierre?"

His face didn't change. "Why not?"

"You don't know who it was shot him? Who might have? No ideas?"

"Plenty idea, but—" With a wave of his hand he gave his ideas to a breeze that had just started up. "I'm in mountains. Five days. Six. Maybe week. Maybe more." He spoke like a man to whom days were a stream, one like another, without definition or date.

There were ten or so other logs piled to the side of the one on the sawbuck, and I tried to figure how long it would take one man to get to the mountains, cut them and trim them, bring them back and unload. One man. Two horses. Eleven logs. X miles. An old grade-school problem popped into my head: If it takes one man ten days to perform a given task, how long will it take ten men, working half-days, to do the same thing? Yeah, and how much wood would a woodchuck chuck—?

Suddenly the breeze turned into gusts, and I could see low thunderheads rising from over the mountains. The weather bureau could do with Pierre.

"Want coffee?" he asked.

"Thanks. I better get back to my car," I said.

It was raining before I reached it, a hard pelt of a rain that was so close to hail that I wondered about crops to the eastward. Lightning jagged down, one bolt so close it barely beat out its own thunder.

Like most thunder showers, this one didn't last long. By the time I braked the car above the picnic grounds, the sky was clear over my head. Everything smelled good to me as I scrambled down the wet ridge. Everything—grass, juniper, scrub pine—breathed revival. The patches of gravel lay polished, each pebble clean and distinct. The sun was low in the west. It had started kindling a cumulus cloud. A good time to fish, to catch that prize cutthroat.

The picnic grounds, that peaceful bottom, looked the same as when I'd last seen it, except that Guy Jamison had taken his chuck wagon out. And except that the rain in its mercy had wiped away the rusty smirch of Buster Hogue's blood.

The peaceful bottom—and on some silver night I could see Buster, dead, haunting the place where a bullet had beaned him, hear him calling out "Who-o?" like an owl as he hunted the ridge.

Then I fished. I fished carefully, used wet flies and dry, all that I had in my book, and even demeaned myself by baiting a plain hook with a grasshopper. But I couldn't get rise or strike from the big trout I'd seen. So I cleaned my catch at the river's edge and then started climbing back up the ridge, using a chance course neither the sheriff nor I had followed before.

If you go hunting arrowheads, go hunting after a rain. There was the reason, the rain, that I found it, a cartridge case, minus bullet, shining copper-bright in a patch of gravel close to the summit.

It was a jacket like none I had seen. Centerfire, to be sure, and reduced as many were at the junction of charge and projectile, but still strange, strange at least to my inexpert eye. On its head, around the cap, was stamped the maker's mark and with it the designation .303 SAV.

I put it in my pocket.

CHAPTER SEVEN

I gulped my supper that night, having so much on my mind. Mother had exclaimed over the nice catch of fish and fed me some warmed-over flank steak with dressing and vegetables she had held back, knowing I would be late. I topped it all off with a piece of chocolate pie, eating it on the run, so to speak.

In dry clothes, with a full stomach, I went looking for the sheriff. He wasn't in his office or at the Bar Star or Commercial Cafe but answered, "Come in," when I knocked at the door of the small apartment he rented in the Jackson Hotel.

It was a pretty neat place, not woman-neat, what with books and magazines spread around, but neater than you'd expect from an old bachelor. He kept spic and span the little kitchen in which he often did his own cooking.

I wondered again that he had never married, at least as far as we knew. He had explained his single state once by saying, "I reckon I've rolled too much to gather a missus." Yes. Rolled over the best moss, I thought.

"Sit down, Jase," he said, motioning toward a hide-covered chair. "What about *Salmo?*"

"Who's he?"

"The trout family."

"Oh, I caught a nice mess, nothing big."

I didn't have fishing on my mind, of course. I had Pierre Chouquette and, more important, the cartridge case in my pocket. My sense of the dramatic told me to mention the case in the third act.

So I told him about my talk with Pierre, told it in

detail while he listened without interrupting. When I had finished, he said, "Small potatoes and few to the hill. That was the crop forecast anyhow, Jase."

"He's so polite but so damn mum."

"Short-spoken, yes, but it doesn't mean anything. He's shy. That's why he lives like a hermit. He doesn't hate people. They just make him uncomfortable. That's my guess."

The thought never had struck me, but it wasn't of any present importance, not when I was about to show what I had found.

Before I could do so, he went on, "There are characters like that, a few, and they get a wrong reputation. Bunch quitters. The opposite of people like, say, Loose Lip Lancaster or, for that matter, even Mabel Main."

"Good night! Have you talked to her?"

"Not lately. Why?"

"I forgot! She stopped me on the street. I got the notion she might have something important to tell you."

"When?"

"Right after the shooting."

The sheriff sighed and said, "All right." He shook his head then, like a man burdened by an uncertain duty.

To the move of his head I said, "I haven't told it all, Sheriff. I fished that big hole by the picnic grounds and came back up the ridge a different way from before."

He looked at me with full attention, maybe suspecting my revelation already.

The center of attraction likes to string things out. "It had rained, you know," I told him. "Good time to spot arrowheads."

He endured me. It flashed in my mind that the twin lines at the sides of his mouth weren't all made by smiles.

I asked, "Guess what I found?"

He wouldn't guess.

Under that pressure my hand dived into my pocket, took out the cartridge case and gave it to him. He studied it for what seemed like minutes. "Yes," he said then. "A Savage three-oh-three. Deer rifle. Long time since I've seen one."

"Is it a clue?"

"What else? About what I had expected, to boot."

He bent his head for a closer look at the case. His hair was beginning to show some gray at the edges. Aloud he asked himself, "A clue, but where does it lead us?"

I answered for him. "We could ask around about who owned one."

"And the owner would say, 'Sure. Take me in.'"

"I mean the neighbors. Those roundabout."

"Who, we would know, weren't the owners themselves." Charleston wasn't being sarcastic. He was just punching holes in my program. "Besides, Jase," he continued, "they're a pretty closed bunch, nearly all with a grudge against Hogue, except Old Man McNair. As for him, he might have one cached away."

"You don't think so."

"Not exactly. But, as the poet said, doth he protest his friendship too much?"

Charleston took a cigar from his pocket, examined it and put it back. "Anyhow, thanks, Jase. The case is a sure-enough clue." He got up and laid it in the drawer of a chest. "Feel like a sandwich or something? I do."

It was our luck to run into Buster Junior and his brother Simon, called Simp, at the Commercial Cafe. The nickname was cruel and too easy. Simple Simon wasn't simple, unless you could call craziness simple. He was a man off to himself, away from the real, in some world his shadowed mind kept creating. When you addressed him, he might explode with a *ho* or a *yah*, or he might explode without provocation; but for the most part he mumbled aloud to himself, in slurred words no one could relate to the going-on conversation. Once in a while, for no reasons at all except for those known to him alone, he would bump, shoving through the people around him, and whoop at those seen or unseen or both. And once in a while, about the time you thought his case was hopeless, he would make sense. He wasn't often brought into town, and, when he was, no one called him Simp, not in the presence of Junior. No, sir.

There were half a dozen other customers in the place, seated and standing, eating and gabbing. Their eyes came to the door as we entered. To the man at his right—Tad Frazier, it was—Buster Junior said, loud enough for everybody to hear, "Salute the flag, boys. Stand up for law and order."

Charleston paid no attention. He took a seat near the door and motioned me to one next to him, and, when Jessie Lou came up the counter to see what we'd have, ordered a ham-and-egg sandwich and coffee. I did the same.

"Law and order," Junior said, again to the company but for our benefit. "In this town the order is for the law to drag ass."

Charleston kept silent, not meaning to goad Junior, I felt sure, but goading him just the same. Junior leaned forward on the counter so as to get a good view of the sheriff. "You hear me up there?"

Before he answered, Charleston took a sip of water from the glass Jessie Lou had set out. "I hear," he said, and gave a little smile to the glass.

"Instead of makin' an arrest," Junior said, speaking to everybody again, "what does he do? He low-rates my old man. Tries to run down his name. As if any son of a bitch could!"

Jessie Lou slid the sandwiches to us, a worried look in her eyes. I could feel an eagerness in the rest, the eagerness of men to see other men fight. The rights of the case didn't matter. Who might win was of secondary importance. Junior's words were fighting words, so let's you two fight.

Charleston took a bite of his sandwich and began chewing thoughtfully.

Junior turned his stare up the counter again. "What you got to say?"

"I'm hungry." After a pause Charleston added, "Let the condemned man eat."

Simp broke out with "Ho" to somebody unseen. The sheriff moved to have a look at him. Simp sat unnoticing, his lips working, as if nothing was happening here to compare with the events of his world.

"If it wasn't for that goddam tin star!" Junior said.

Charleston went on eating.

It began to look like no contest, with Junior the winner by default, to the general disappointment. With everybody else quiet, Simp's mumbles sounded plain, but mysterious.

Charleston ate the last of his sandwich, took a sip of coffee, wiped his mouth and turned on his stool. His voice was mild. "I'd like to talk to you, Junior."

"Talk. Talk! Jesus Christ! Talk about what?"

"Maybe about what makes you a damn fool." The tone was still soft.

Junior lunged off his stool and charged up. For a minute I thought he would swing, star or no star. Charleston looked in his eyes, not moving, his face composed. In the end I think it was that very control that got Junior. It fazes you, at the moment of action, to face a man who sits calm, not angry but not afraid either. Anyhow, Junior didn't swing. He held on to his storm long enough for a last bolt. "Talk! I'm a son of a bitch!"

Charleston nodded, to either the first or the second part of Junior's reply or to both. "Then, later, who knows? No rule says I have to take my star to bed with me."

"Meanin'?"

"Just what you think. Let's go to the office."

Junior turned slowly, like a man just reconciling himself to a compromise, and commanded, "Simon! Come on."

Simp yelled, "Ho!" loud enough to be heard down the block, left his stool and came toward us.

I got up as Charleston did.

Junior said, pointing to me, "He goin' to play catch with us?"

"Want to bring your sandwich along, Jase?" Charleston asked. That answered that, though I abandoned the sandwich.

We went out, the four of us, leaving a rising chatter behind us. There would be talk about where the fight would be if there was one.

In the office the sheriff motioned us all to seats after I had brought in a chair. He let himself down at his desk. Old Jimmy poked his head through the rear door, announced he had nothing to report and asked if it was all right if he went. A man who's known everything has no curiosity left.

Charleston started easily. "Two things first, Junior. One, I'm after the man that shot your father. Second, I haven't downgraded him. If I mentioned his deal with Ben Day, it was only in the hope it would help me locate the sniper. I did mention it, to old McNair. That's who told you. You and I know, so do others, that the deal was on the shady side. That doesn't matter now."

"The goddam Forest Service."

"All right. I've talked to most of the people present at the picnic, I admit with no results. I can't even guess yet. I need your help. Let's start with McNair."

"Old Taller-Ass is our friend. Good reasons, but I wouldn't tell you even if I knew all of it."

"No need to. Statute of limitations applies to everything except murder."

Charleston picked up a pencil and studied it. While he studied, Simp muttered, his eyes blank. Charleston's gaze flicked to him before he went on. "Obligations," he said. "Sometimes they weigh on a man."

"What do you mean by that?"

"Like losing a friend by loaning him money."

"Nuts! McNair is an ornery old bastard all right, but you're on the wrong horse."

"I'm not on him. I'm just sizing him up."

Simp blurted out, "Yah," not to second the motion.

"People I haven't seen, Jase and I," Charleston went on. He was making pencil marks on his blotter. "Professor Powell Hawthorne, for one."

"Stuck-up son of a bitch. Goes for his girl, too, or part of it."

"You know them well?"

"Not well but enough. Christ, she wouldn't speak to you if you were the last man on earth."

Charleston's eyes lifted to Junior. I wondered if he was wondering the same thing that I was, even if Junior did have a wife.

Junior hitched in his chair. "Shut up, Simon!"

Simon answered, "Yo," and went on jabbering. Charleston was looking at him.

"To me it's not so goddam mysterious," Junior said, hitching back.

"You mean Ben Day?"

"Well?"

"On the face of it, yes," Charleston answered, making more marks on the blotter. "That's the trouble. Too obvious. Whatever Day is, the first thing is cagey. Unlikely to put his foot in a plain-to-see trap. Yes or no?"

"I could see myself doin' it, bein' Day."

"Sure. But you aren't. Let's get on. Doctor Ulysses Pierpont? We haven't seen him."

"That fake!"

"Oh?"

"What I mean is—what the truth is—anyone says he can cure what's wrong in a head is loco himself. Or a damn cheat."

"Seems you know him?"

"Some. He came to the ranch once, all polite business. What he wanted was to buy land off us. We laughed at him. Hell, we don't sell land, we buy it, and so we laughed. Later on—"

"Later on, what?"

"Nothin'. He don't wear well."

Charleston heaved in a breath and sighed it out. "I guess that's all, Junior. But I aim to find that sniper. I aim to bring him in, no matter who he is or who sets up a howl. Got that? That what you want?"

"Well, of course, sure I do."

"If I don't, I'll turn in my badge. That's a promise."

As if reminded, he took his star off, laid it on his desk and looked at Junior, his eyes questioning.

It took Junior a minute, but finally he said, "I don't guess so. Not now, anyhow." Then for the first time he got my sympathy by saying, "It's my own father."

"I know."

Junior got up and motioned to Simp, who might

as well have been in the next county for all the attention he paid.

"By the way," the sheriff asked, "you happen to own a Savage three-oh-three?"

Junior looked puzzled. "We did once. I guess it's still lyin' around the ranch somewhere, maybe in the bunkhouse. Why?"

It was then that Simp sprang his fit. He came out of his chair as if goosed, shouting commands or alarms to his unseen company, and lunged for the door, knocking Junior half out of his chair.

Junior said, "Simon. Now, Simon. Easy, boy."

But Simp charged from the office, still howling, and Junior went after him.

We sat still, the sheriff and I, and after a while, from far down the hall, heard Simp say, "Please, Junior, isn't it time to go home?"

"Psychological," Charleston said then. "Out of my reach."

I doubted it was and knew later it wasn't.

He went on, "First thing in the morning I'll call Doctor Pierpont and ask him to drop in soon as he can."

"About Simp?"

All Charleston answered was, "Pitiful."

CHAPTER EIGHT

From the protection of a sheep panel Ben Day was shooting at me. I could see him through the slats, sneaking from one position to another, and could see the rifle poking through. It was a Savage .303. Against the gun I had a baseball, but I couldn't throw it, wild or true. My arm hung paralyzed.

Day called as he aimed, "Now, boy," but it was my

father speaking. Through the mists I heard him add, "I thought you'd want to get up, son. It's pretty late." His hand tousled my hair.

I rolled over. "Thanks, Dad," I said. "My arm's asleep." I waved it and rubbed it with my other hand. "Thanks double. I was having a bad dream."

"Well you might," he told me. "Buster Hogue is dead, according to the radio."

I came fast out of bed. "So now it's murder!"

He said, "I fear so," and left my room, shaking his head. He would rather I pitched ball than pried into crime. On the mound a man could get shelled: history couldn't cite a case in which one had been shot.

Only Halvor Amussen was in the sheriff's office, working the day shift so's he'd have the night off. He was a big man, big enough to eat hay, and I often wondered about his well-known if unauthenticated exploits in bed. It was hard to picture him wrestling on a regulation four-poster.

He told me the sheriff was attending a sheriff's sale out in the country but had learned about Buster Hogue's death before setting out. "A blessing, I call it," Halvor said. "What the hell? Who wants to live without brains?"

"Lots of people do and seem to like it all right."

"Uppity, are you?" he asked. "But, looking at you, I guess you're right."

There was nothing to do except wait for lunch and the sheriff's return later on. So I spent some time in what I thought of as thought. Suspects? Old Man McNair, whom Charleston showed some unaccountable interest in. Loose Lancaster, who reported Hogue had taken off a hat later shown to be punctured. Plenty Toogood was out. He couldn't see to drive, let alone aim a rifle by moonlight. Out too, I supposed, were Blue Piatt and Oscar Oliphant, whom Charleston had talked to the night I rolled the hearse to the hospital. No need to think about Guy Jamison and his dudes. Ben Day? Unlikely. Too cagey. Chouquette? Small potatoes and few to the hill. Though we hadn't talked to either, to suspect the psychiatrist or the professor was to need a psychiatrist's help. In my mind it all simmered down to Simp Hogue, that crazy, lost bastard. Motive? One of his secret own that made no sense to sane men.

Having solved the case, I decided to write a report of all that had gone on, beginning with Buster Hogue's delivery by truck. A straining of memory, you might think, but it wasn't, not much. In my old-fashioned grade school, where you were required to memorize line after line after line of pieces the English teacher thought great, I won steady A's without effort. Things read or heard imprinted themselves on my mind, there to stay. I can't see any special, personal benefit in being able to recite "Evangeline" or "The Man with the Hoe" or "The Lady of Shalott" line by line without a bobble, but the faculty of remembering served me well in making out the report, which I left unfinished and hidden at lunchtime. I would go on with it later. Until after completion, no one, Charleston particularly, was to see it.

The sheriff returned to the office at 1:30 by the clock on the wall, said hello, he was tied up for a while, but would I like to take a trip later on, say, after supper? I said I would and, wondering how to spend a long afternoon, assembled my fingerprinting kit and took it home. Whenever Halvor saw me working with it, he addressed me as Sherlock or Hawkshaw.

Along the street and in the Commercial Cafe, where I stopped for a Coke, as well as in the post office and Bar Star, I supposed, people were talking and shaking their heads, saying, even those who had not liked him too well, it was too bad Buster Hogue had kicked off. A good man, Hogue, whatever his not-mentioned failings. A solid Republican who had never sought office, a man who gave of himself and his cash to causes thought worthy. For years a member of the state central committee, from which his work for sound party policy had been felt far and wide. A good man, yep, and too bad. Everybody's loss.

Ranchers and cowtowns are generally Republican, which partly accounted for the general sentiment. Irrigation districts and wheat elevators mark the Democrats' habitats, where the blight of government interference is promoted. Once, having been smarted up by a teacher, I asked a cattleman if the tariff wasn't government interference. It wasn't.

A shower came up while I walked, and I hurried on home, where Mother remarked that a beef stew wasn't a beef stew without the rutabagas she couldn't find in the stores.

In my room I fiddled with my fingerprinting kit. It included an ink pad, paper, lifting tape, powder and brush, but not the camera that would have accompanied a costlier set. There was in the room, in addition, a book on fingerprint classification that the FBI had sent me on being assured of my interest. To date I hadn't got far with it.

After experiments, using a square of glass for the purpose, I lifted a couple of pretty fair sets of my own prints.

My old man came from the office a little later, and we ate. Both he and I thought the stew was damn good, though neither of us used the adjective, it being as contrary to his principles as the stew was agreeable to his taste.

When we were done, I said I might be out late, seeing as I was going on a trip with the sheriff.

"To where?" my dad asked.

"He didn't tell me."

"Keep in mind," he said, "that a murder has been committed. The guilty man wouldn't hesitate at a second."

Mother chimed in. "Must you go?"

"Theirs not to reason why. Theirs but to do and die," I answered, and tried to ease my mother's worry with a good-bye kiss.

I went to the sheriff's office and waited. It was at long light, with the sky bright but the sun itself lost over the mountains, that Charleston came in and asked was I ready.

God knows I was.

On the way to the Special I asked him, "Where to?" but all he answered was, "West."

So we tooled out the highway and took that rocky-assed road again. We were keeping it hot, no matter how cold the trail grew. After the shower the air was newborn. Even the engine enjoyed it, purring along as if heaven had sent just the right mixture. The mountains scalloped the western sky as if scissored. Our dust rose lazily behind us and settled to rest. If there were sermons in stones, there was music in this quiet hour, music accompanied by the soft throb of the motor and the low drum of wheels against gravel. Neither of us spoke.

It wasn't until we turned to the right off the road and crossed a cattle guard into a lane that I knew where we were going. To Professor Powell Hawthorne's. That was where. I had identified him—and her—by asking, as if I didn't care, who was that duded-up old gent with the whiskers who had showed up at the ball game.

There were lights in the house, friendly lights that beamed into the gathering dark. A dog came out of somewhere to welcome us. You could tell from his bark that he wouldn't bite.

We eased to a stop and got out, and a door opened, and the professor stood there with his Vandyke and raised a hand in salute. "Come in, Mr. Charleston," he said, "you and your deputy. It was kind of you to phone first." As I came into fuller light, he went on, "Don't I recognize you? Yes. The ballplayer."

"Jason Beard," I told him.

He shook hands with Charleston and me and motioned us in. The girl was there. She was what I noticed at first. She was all I noticed.

Though nearly every one of them does on occasion, not many women can wear slacks without discouraging masculine interest. Too bulgy in front or too broad behind, or both, they suggest unbaked bread dough on the high rise. But she wore them and didn't. She had on, too, a bright blouse, mostly red, that showed she was female all right. Yet there was more to her than shape. There was a sort of radiance, like a dimmed light that could be switched to high beam.

"Marguerite," the professor said, "I don't think you have met Sheriff Charleston or Jason—"

I helped him with "Beard."

"My daughter, gentlemen. I call her Geet for short, disliking the common Maggie."

She nodded nicely and on second thought came to us and offered a hand. It was strong enough but small and short-fingered for the Little Leagues.

The room we were in—the lodge room, he called it later—struck me as just right. Not big, not small, well-furnished but not cluttered, it showed easy taste. It had a beamed ceiling and a native-stone fireplace in which a just kindled fire worked on aspen twigs. Against the end wall facing me was a high, solid-fronted cabinet with double locks. I saw a picture of Geet and one of an oil well gone wild. A coffee table supported books and magazines. They looked technical.

After we were seated and had talked about the weather and what-not and the professor had mentioned my pitching approvingly, he asked if we wouldn't like some refreshments. He and the sheriff settled for bourbon and water. I said I wasn't thirsty or hungry, either, though Geet brought in soft drinks and some home-made cookies that I could have gobbled.

The sheriff picked up and examined a piece of stone that had been laid out with others on a small stand table close to his chair. "I confess with regret," he said in his best manner, "that I know little about your profession, Professor."

"I haven't been teaching for years, so the 'professor' is—shall we say—vestigial," Mr. Hawthorne said after a thoughtful sip from his glass. "I suppose I'm still a geologist, but no longer a petroleum geologist. No longer. No."

"No?"

"They are on my conscience, my ecological conscience, the oil fields I was instrumental in finding. That work, those findings, have enabled me to retire, and so I shouldn't complain, I suppose, but sometimes I have the feeling I am living on the proceeds of wrongdoing." He gestured toward the picture of the oil well gone wild. "There is a reminder of my leisure and my sin. Blessings have their price."

Though I came of a good family myself, I was about

to decide he was too fine-haired for me. Who in hell didn't dream of striking oil?

Charleston nodded and smiled. The girl's eyes were on him as he spoke. "I know a cattle rancher who curses the day oil was found on his land. An ex-rancher, I should say. But I doubt that stockholders and General Motors share your sentiment."

Mr. Hawthorne dismissed them with a wave of his hand. "Now I am far more interested in the history of earth. How it came to be. How it grew through the ages. What flora and fauna it supported in the years of its becoming. So I study and think and look and now and then gather a stone. Call me a rock hound, a fossil lover, a seeker of evidence of things, circumstances, creatures long vanished."

As speeches go, it seemed a pretty good speech, though rather airy. Good or bad, it was heightened or excused by the felt presence of Geet. No common-run father could have fathered her.

"I am done with the exploitation of earth," the professor went on. "Much better to do what Geet is doing. Next year she will have her degree in zoology. The order of Lepidoptera is her immediate interest."

It must have been my look of ignorance that caused the girl to explain, "Butterflies and such."

All right. Butterflies and such. But here she was about to get a college degree when I had yet to earn my high-school diploma. That difference removed her yet made her more fetching. I told myself there was no rule against catching up.

"But you didn't come to hear me talk about myself," Mr. Hawthorne said abruptly.

"No, Charleston answered, "though your views are worth listening to, more interesting in the long haul than murder." He smiled his easy smile. "With an oil well or two to my credit, I could dismiss the sins of others and concentrate on my own."

Geet laughed.

"You know Hogue is dead," Charleston continued. "How well were you acquainted with him?"

"We met a time or two. You may have heard he

tried to buy my place, offering twice what it would bring on the market but not a fraction of its worth to me. He couldn't understand my refusal."

"And you had words?"

"The tender of an offer and its rejection can hardly be managed without utterance."

A case or two flashed in my mind in which both had been managed with not a word said. Charleston was looking at the professor, without utterance conveying a message.

The girl broke in. "Father, you're being precious."

He gave her a small, benign smile. "Perhaps I am, my dear."

But the tone was set despite the admission, a tone I didn't like there in Geet's presence.

Charleston said, "You had words, then."

"We didn't quarrel, if that's what you mean. Not really quarrel. It was hard for him to comprehend that some things existed beyond the embrace of his money."

"And that was all?"

"Not quite, if I am to make a clean breast of things, as you men of the law might put it. Hogue is—was—in possession of a piece of land on which rises a spring that feeds my pond here. He indicated, without actually threatening, that he might cut off the water supply unless I sold out."

"That's enough for a quarrel."

"No. My water right is secure. I know it. He knew it, I'm sure. Ours wasn't an altercation. An altercation implies real heat. We just talked, admittedly not as friends."

"All right." Charleston was insisting on being all business. "Now someone somewhere in this neighborhood shot Buster Hogue. Can you help me at all? How well do you know your neighbors?"

"Far from well. Possibly you can except the Jamisons, brief as our acquaintance has been. Most of the rest I met for the first time at that unhappy picnic." He looked at the empty glasses and said, "Geet, would you bring us another drink, please?"

In her absence Charleston went on. "McNair?

Lancaster? The Hogue brothers? Ben Day? What do you know about them? About any one? Any least little thing that might have a bearing?"

"No help. Nothing. Very little hearsay, even. You see, Sheriff, we live pretty well apart, Geet and I. It's a rare day we're not off in the fields and the hills, pursuing our interests. It's not that we shun society. We don't have much time for it. And you must remember we are very recent arrivals here."

Geet brought the drinks in, on a tray naturally, since she had class. Both men thanked her, and she sat down, saying nothing.

"As educated men, though in different fields, I would imagine you and Doctor Ulysses Pierpont have much in common," the sheriff said. "Are you acquainted?"

Abruptly the girl said, "We know him."

"Slightly, only slightly," her father answered before she could go on. "But I venture to say, Sheriff, that you are wrong about common interests."

The girl's gaze went to Charleston. "His manner toward Father was insulting, there at the picnic, when Father rushed to help poor Mr. Hogue. As if Father, himself a scientist, didn't know the rudiments of first aid."

"Now, now, Geet," Professor Hawthorne said. "It's no doubt that he feels perhaps just a little cool toward me since I refused to sell him this place." He addressed Charleston then. "You know he wanted to buy it, or at least part of it?"

At Charleston's nod Professor Hawthorne returned to common interests, or the lack of them. "Psychiatry, insofar as I have observed it, is an all-absorbing involvement, a specialty with little elbow room for other concerns, which is not to denigrate Doctor Pierpont or the profession. He is, I assume, a highly competent practitioner. Degrees like his are hard-won."

"I had a date with him once," the girl said, as if clinging to a point that was being abandoned.

Charleston answered, "Oh?"

"Once was enough. Once was too many." She made a small flinging-away gesture.

"Now, Geet," her father said, "your dates, or date, are hardly germane to this inquiry."

"All right, but he's impossible. Such delusions!"

"Of grandeur?" Charleston asked.

"Delusions of the illusion of grandeur."

Professor Hawthorne smiled and said in the soft tones of fatherhood, "Your character analysis is remarkable in view of the brief association."

She smiled in return and answered, "It's a gift, Father—the voices I hear."

"Uh-huh. And if, by your confusing abstractions, you mean the man has ambitions, then hurrah for him. At his age he should have."

Charleston had listened with a sort of alert amusement but now, apparently having had enough of Dr. Pierpont, abruptly changed the subject. "You deal in old firearms, Mr. Hawthorne?"

"'Deal' is hardly the word for a hobby. I collect rare pieces, some by barter, some by outright purchase. Collecters are a breed to themselves, Mr. Charleston. *Sui generis*, you might say. Some specialize in short arms, some in long, some in muzzle loaders, some in military arms. In acquiring what they want, in trading, that is, they often accept additional items of little interest to them but of some little, or perhaps great, interest to other collectors. These constitute their trading stock."

He lifted his glass. He seemed to be enjoying himself, as much with his hobby as he had with earth's history. He waved toward the closed and locked cabinet. "My aim has been to collect pieces that reflect progress in arms-making, those and the rifles, or muskets, that relate to given periods and certain events. They overlap often, of course. In that cabinet is a Sharps used in the Battle of Adobe Wells and a Springfield fired by a trooper of Custer's on the Little Bighorn, both well authenticated. I have a fine Henry, a first-year Winchester and a number of Kentuckys, more properly called Pennsylvanias. But why go on?"

Charleston forged on. "You were talking trade recently."

"Why, yes. By telephone."

It came to me then that Charleston had seen Mabel Main.

"A collector in Louisville, Kentucky, has a very fine Hawken," the professor continued. "It is one of the very few extant and one of fewer that has not been mutilated by amateurs. The Hawken was the fur-hunter's rifle, you know."

He laughed and said, "Let me digress. I had a time making connections by phone. We are on a party line here, as you are aware. More properly it could be called a mass line. There is one instrument in particular, that of a widow and her two teen-age daughters, that is in operation incessantly, to the frustration of all the rest of us on the line. They were talking, of course, when I wished to put through my call. They talked, and they talked, but I outwitted them finally. There is an electric outlet close to my phone. I plugged into it an old, clattery shaver, lifted the receiver and let it clatter in the transmitter." He laughed again. "That did for the wenches, as I choose to call them. No doubt they're blaming the telephone company now, which doesn't bother me in the slightest."

"You're giving yourself away, Father," the girl said. "I could take that statement two ways."

"Oh, well." He shrugged. "But back to the Hawken, Mr. Charleston. The owner's prime interest is short arms, and just recently I've come into possession of some very good ones. I thought I might make a trade. It disappointed me that I didn't." As if the thought had just come to him, he added, "That call. Not much escapes you, does it?"

The girl's gaze was on the sheriff, as it had been during most of the conversation. Did it betray reserve, opposition, unwilling interest? I couldn't tell.

Charleston asked, "Are you acquainted with the Savage three-oh-three?"

"Surely. Deer rifle. It's becoming somewhat scarce but not sufficiently rare yet to tempt real collectors. Matter of fact, I have one, not important enough to lock in the cabinet and in poor condition besides. It's too loose in the breach for safe firing. Possibility of a blow-back, you understand."

"May I see it?"

"Of course." Mr. Hawthorne turned to his daughter. "Geet, will you bring it out of the storeroom?"

She disappeared, only to return in a minute and report, "It's not there, Father."

"Not there? Of course it is, stacked along with the Harper's Ferry and Hudson's Bay muskets."

"That's where I looked."

Mr. Hawthorne got up with an abrupt, "Excuse me." The girl followed him out as if to prove her point. Charleston sat, with nothing in his face I could read.

"I can't understand it," Mr. Hawthorne said as he and Geet came back to the room. "I know I stored it there. Now who would steal that old piece?" He paused. "I gather that a three-oh-three is important to your investigation?"

The sheriff said, "Yes."

"If anyone fired that old gun, he may have powder burns on him."

"You say you are gone from the house a great deal. Do you lock the place up?"

"My name may suggest the east, Mr. Charleston, but my heritage is early western. So I never lock doors."

"Except those to your gun cabinet."

"The one exception. Gun fanciers aren't to be trusted. I'm lucky, even so, that so far I've lost only the Savage."

"You know its number?"

"Naturally." Mr. Hawthorne stepped to a desk, slid back a drawer and answered while he read from a page. "It's Model eighteen ninety-nine, number one-four-seven-one-four-nine."

Charleston had taken a pad from his pocket and made note of the description. Now he stood up. "Thank you for your help."

"Help? You don't think—"

"Seldom if ever. Thanks to you, too, Miss Marguerite, and good night to you both."

I followed with my thank-yous, not that they got much attention.

Leaving, Charleston turned back to say, "You may just have mislaid it. If it turns up, will you let me know?" Assured that they would, he led along to the Special.

Ours was mostly a silent trip home. What kept me quiet, what fretted me, wasn't the matter of murder and what clues we had picked up, if any. It was the toney manner of Mr. Hawthorne. It was him and that beautiful daughter of his. On close acquaintance would I find her as affected as he had appeared? Like father like daughter? Come to think of it, he and Buster Hogue, if different in their ways, had a quality in common. That was the assurance, the touch of superiority, the assumption of specialty that money generates in some men. And now I remembered from my reading the source of that double-jointed adjective that had occurred to me earlier. It came from a bit of verse left by Black Bart, the California bandit, after he had held up a stagecoach.

> *I've labored long and hard for bread,*
> *For honor and for riches,*
> *But on my toes too long you've tred,*
> *You fine-haired sons of bitches.*

Out of the silence Charleston said, "You seem a mite fidgety, Jase. Look in the jockey box and get your mind on your business."

I opened the glove compartment, as easterners call it, and found a new baseball. It felt good to a hand that had too long neglected its duty.

Near town Charleston remarked as if to himself, "Damn likely girl," and that was the end of our conversation until we gave each other good night.

CHAPTER NINE

Dr. Ulysses Pierpont was not at all what his name suggested. I had expected to see a large and stately man with wisdom written deep in his face. Or possibly a modern version of General Ulysses S. Grant, whose ability would be flavored with booze. But Dr. Pierpont turned out to be a rather small man with a trim mustache, a pointed gray gaze, a flat stomach and clothes that spelled tailor-made. "Spruce" was a word for him.

We, the sheriff and I, were in his apartment when a quiet knock came at the door. After Charleston had opened it, I heard the visitor say, "Good evening. I came as soon as I conveniently could. Doctor Ulysses Pierpont, and you are Sheriff Charleston, I suppose. Your man at the office said I might find you here."

The sheriff made him welcome.

Charleston and I had eaten supper at his place, enjoying steaks that a grateful rancher had provided after Charleston had collared a shoot-and-run rustler who had made off with a beef. An evening chill had set in, and Charleston had just closed a window when the knock sounded.

After some little talk about nothing much, the sheriff told Dr. Pierpont, "I thought you might help me. About the murder, of course. I can pick up clues, if there are any, and I can make deductions, right or wrong. I've even been known to have some hunches as to human behavior. But in this case there are no clues, no deductions, no hunches. I'm stumped."

Dr. Pierpont turned his sharp gray gaze on me and shifted it back to the sheriff. He was asking, I felt sure, whether I had a proper part here. Charleston answered yes with his silence.

"I fail to understand," Dr. Pierpont said. "After Mr. Hogue was shot at the picnic, I treated him as best I was able. I had and I have no idea who the marksman might be." Dr. Pierpont spoke briskly, but after consideration, as if his thoughts had to be well shaped before voiced. "I have little acquaintance with those at the picnic, and, needless to say, I'm not a detective. How then may I help?"

"My barnyard psychology isn't up to the mark," Charleston answered, smiling. "Sheriffs aren't elected for brains, Doctor Pierpont. They get into office because they're hail-fellow-well-met, or maybe they've come out top dog in a fight. So, knowing my limits, I thought to extend them by talking to you."

Dr. Pierpont didn't smile in return. He listened as if to a troubled patient and waited for more.

"I want an expert's insight. I want to know what a given character is capable of and what he isn't. I want to ask you some questions about people, not necessarily suspects."

"Surely you don't expect me to answer offhand? I fear what you hope from me requires a knowledge of personalities that I don't possess. And if I did, professionally I couldn't divulge it."

"We will treat the questions and answers as confidential, Doctor, and, more than that, hypothetical when that is demanded. You are acquainted with Simon Hogue, son of Buster?"

"Obviously you know he was my patient."

Charleston considered. "No," he said, "I did not know that. Nobody does."

"Then I'm sorry."

Into a moment's pause Charleston said, "I forgot to offer you a drink. What will it be?"

"A small whiskey, if you have it. No water or ice." The drink seemed appropriate to the man.

I got up and went to the kitchen. Charleston liked water mixed with his bourbon.

When I returned, Charleston was saying, "No

harm done, Doctor. It's plain to all that Simon needs help. The news that he's been to you, if ever released, couldn't cinch a case already cinched."

"An inexcusable stigma still often attaches to those who seek the aid of psychiatry." The doctor took a sip of his whiskey. "As if everybody, worldwide, on occasion didn't need therapy."

"Granted," Charleston replied. "I figure all of us are a little bit crazy, and some of us crazier. than that some of the time."

"'Crazy' is not a term I use."

"No. What would you say about Simon Hogue?"

"I can say this much, now that I've said as much as I have. I had six meetings with the boy. I thought he showed improvement and would show more. But Buster Hogue, his father, became disgusted that I hadn't performed an instant miracle and terminated the treatments."

"Again, what about Simon?"

"I dislike classifications, as if all mental and emotional disturbances could be sorted, labeled and pigeonholed. You call him crazy, others would say insane, still others perhaps feeble-minded. Psychiatry has its own terminology, but no term is exact." Dr. Pierpont took a last sip of his drink as if to aid in his phrasing. "Let us just say, loosely again, that he suffers from schizophrenia."

"Here is the question in my mind," Charleston went on. "Could a boy, or a man if you please, plan and carry out a shooting—a man or a boy so afflicted, I mean? And a shooting like Buster Hogue's, I mean, too?"

Dr. Pierpont gave thought to the question, his slim, keen face lost in the answer. Then he replied, "This is hypothetical, as you say. Let me get away from Simon. Let me generalize. Then I shall have to give a qualified yes. It is not impossible that a man so out of touch with reality—no reference to Simon, understand—could plot and perform such a crime. We see stranger things, we in the profession."

The sheriff finished his drink, and I went out to the kitchen for refills. But I could still hear.

"Thanks," the sheriff was saying out of my sight.

"That's one thing I know or at least must consider. But motive? Can you tell me, without ethical strain, whether Simon disliked or hated his father?"

I came back in, served the drinks and sat down.

"No strain because there is nothing to divulge," Dr. Pierpont replied. "It was difficult to get anything at all out of Simon. But if I may speak generally again, I'll tell you what you already know. Most sons harbor an antagonism, latent or active, for their fathers." He added after a silence, "Perhaps, among other influences, that feeling is proportionate to the success of the father."

Charleston found cigars, offered one to Dr. Pierpont, who let it be lighted under the line of his mustache, and then fired up himself. He asked, along with a puff of smoke, "How well did you know Buster Hogue?"

"Not really well, but well enough."

"Just from talking about his son, I suppose?"

"And one other instance. I tried to buy a few acres from him to add to my own."

"No sale, huh?"

"None. He seemed to think the proposal ridiculous. I thought he was, and so both of us had a laugh." The doctor tapped a little ash off his cigar, being careful to see that it hit an ashtray.

"Even so, afterward he came to you about Simon?"

"Yes. Afterward. But why these questions, Sheriff?"

Charleston waved one hand, indicating the questions were pointless. "Just trying to get a line on Hogue. You haven't told me just what kind of a man he seemed to you."

"I tend away from surface opinions. He was never a patient of mine."

"But I didn't suggest a professional judgment. Make it lay, clerical, secular, whatever."

Dr. Pierpont weighed his answer. "I suppose I could say he struck me as rather arrogant. I can well imagine he made enemies. But men of means often assume the mantle of superiority."

"Isn't that the truth," Charleston said.

"Unhappily I encounter a good many of them in my practice. Any psychiatrist does."

"And any man without money who runs up against money."

"Yes." The doctor sipped and continued gravely, "Wealth. The arrogance it creates and the power it bestows." He blew out a brief breath at the thought.

Charleston put in mildly, "In the wrong hands, you mean, Doctor?"

"Where so much of it is. Wealth, and consequently position and influence. Consequently a circle of toadies, too. Power misplaced."

"Direct cause and effect?" Charleston added.

"You answer your own question, Sheriff." Of a sudden Dr. Pierpont, who had looked dead serious an instant before, relaxed and smiled for the first time. "I've been talking pointlessly, maundering really, far from my field of competence. Forgive me."

"I was agreeing."

And so, I thought, was I. Wealth in the wrong hands, in the hands of the solely greedy, and with it the influence that money exerted. I could cite a few samples myself and felt like saying thanks to the doctor for enforcing my young and hesitant judgments.

Charleston pointed toward the glasses, not speaking, and I got up for more drinks.

"Professor Powell Hawthorne seems quite different," Charleston was saying. "You've met him, I'm sure."

"Oh, yes. I tried to buy land from him, too, unsuccessfully."

"And what, if you'll tell me, was your impression of him?"

While Dr. Pierpont formulated his answer, I brought in the drinks and sat down.

"First impressions are so often wrong, but, frankly, I found him a little too lofty, too precious, for my taste. Not arrogant, though, unless a certain affectation is arrogance."

So, it dodged in my head, the doctor felt as I did, though his language was better. Professor Hawthorne was too fine-haired even if he was the father of Geet.

I gathered the interview was closing when Charleston asked, "Are you going on up to your place tonight?"

"Heavens, no," Dr. Pierpont replied. "Today is, let me see, Wednesday. I have a full day at the office tomorrow and even today had to crowd myself to drive up to see you now."

"I appreciate it. I don't imagine you have leisure enough to enjoy your place to the full?"

"Not nearly. Only about once a month. Oh, occasionally I sneak an afternoon and evening off, as I did the day of the picnic, though I had no advance notice of it, being more or less an outsider."

Now that he was off the professional reservation, now that whiskey had warmed him, the doctor was being more fluent. "Later, soon I vow, I'll make more time for myself. I have plans, Sheriff, plans for something considerably more than a mere cabin. And somehow I'll add to my acreage. You must come to see me then."

"I'll be happy to," Charleston replied. "Will you have another drink, Doctor?"

Dr. Pierpont looked at his wrist watch. "Thanks, no. Time's up. I must get back to the city."

He rose from his chair, as we did from ours, and shook hands with both of us. He had a good grip and looked a man in the eye—which recommended him to me. As he closed the door, he said, "I'm sorry the profession seems to be useless to you."

The sheriff came back to his chair, slumped in it and asked, "Well, Jase?"

I had gone to the front window and was looking out and down. "He struck me as all right. Scrupulous about Simon Hogue. And about wealth, I was with him."

"Smart man," Charleston said.

"Hey," I told him, still with my face to the window, "he's sure got a flashy car. Foreign job, I bet."

"So?"

I turned toward him. "You didn't tell him about the three-oh-three casing."

"Sometimes damn if I don't seem to forget—which is just as well, I reckon. Anyhow, doesn't matter." Charleston grinned a tired grin. "See you tomorrow, Jase."

I took the hint.

CHAPTER TEN

Thursday, a week since Buster Hogue had been potted, and no arrests yet and no likely ones without evidence we didn't have.

The sheriff was busy with paperwork when I entered the office. He hated it, as I knew, and he looked out of place at a desk with a clutter of pages to be read, signed and answered. A man like him, with a face written on by wind and sun and a body shaped by the outdoors, belonged in the open.

Later on, he said, he would give some dictation to Jody Lester, a stenographer the office shared with that of the county clerk. And he'd better stick around, he told me, to deliver a fugitive to an officer from the eastern part of the state. The prisoner, collared by Halvor Amussen, was wanted for storehouse breaking, check forging, car theft and a few other little things abhorred by the law and was to be returned to the scene of his crimes.

Still later, Charleston went on, he was going to Buster Hogue's funeral, set for two o'clock at the Methodist church.

So there was no work for me. Before I dragged away, though, the sheriff pushed the papers aside and leaned back. Jimmy Conner came in from the jail at about the same time.

"Well, boys," Charleston asked, "any answers today?"

"About who killed Buster Hogue?"

"About anything. People want answers, Jase, certain-sure answers, of which there ain't so many in stock."

Jimmy said, "There's a lot of questions never been

71

answered. Like why roses smell sweetest when well fed with shit."

"Don't strain yourself, Jimmy. That's what the little hen said to the big hen when the big hen bragged that her eggs brought a nickel more on the dozen. Wasn't worth the wear and tear."

"The wear and tear in the Hogue case is getting the evidence," I put in. "What we know all points one way."

Charleston lighted a cigar and leaned farther back. "Does it, Jase? Maybe. I don't know. But answers? Let me tell you. There's a town close to my old home down south of here, and a drummer, making his first visit, came to the place on a train. When he got off at the station, he saw the settlement was a half-mile away, and no means of getting there but by walkin'."

The sheriff drew on his cigar as if giving us time to get the picture. "Well, the drummer looked at the long hike he'd have to take, and he looked at his heavy sample case, and he looked at his feet.

"It happened old Gary Watkins was loafin' on the platform, which was his habit, and the drummer asked him, 'Why did they build the station so far from the town?'"

"'I dunno,' Gary says, taking his pipe out of his mouth. 'I dunno, unless they wanted it close to the tracks.'"

Jimmy laughed, along with me, and said, "I don't see where that takes us."

"Nowhere, I reckon," Charleston told us, and blew out a thoughtful plume of smoke. "Nowhere, maybe, except away from wrong-put questions and smart-ass answers."

I felt perhaps he had gigged me for being sure Simp Hogue had knocked off his father, but I didn't say anything. I took my baseball and wandered downtown, wishing Terry was on hand to play catch with. He was with a crew fighting a forest fire that laid a low haze over the mountains.

Felix Underwood came out of his parlors, powdered and dressed for the Hogue ceremony. He was the coroner and had spoken against the idea of an inquest, saying, "Hell, he got shot, didn't he? By a person or persons unknown? How you going to improve on what's plain on its face?"

I went home and made a few throws at the barn door, not putting much heart into them. Anyway, my arm felt good, good enough for the home game on Sunday. My father came to the house for lunch and later dressed for the funeral. I begged off from going to it, not because I didn't like Hogue but because the preacher sure as hell would commend his soul to heaven and take a long time in presenting credentials. Reverend Hauser, having the ear of God, believed in chewing it to a frazzle.

I wandered down to Main Street. There weren't many people about, and those that were were mostly dressed sober, as was fitting when a good citizen was to be laid down for good. But Dippy Ferguson hadn't heard about the funeral and wore his shirt open under a jacket that would have stampeded a blind horse. Under his arm he carried an old, crush-type folder that held order blanks or samples or exhibits of whatever he chanced to be selling.

Dippy was a wandering salesman who visited our town only once in a while. I had known him to sell, or try to sell, door to door, combination glass cutters and knife sharpeners, extracts, custom suits, off-beat vacuum cleaners and thousand-proof vitamins not available in any drugstore. Right now his line was magazines and newspapers or, rather, subscriptions to them.

He didn't do badly, not with the low-priced stuff, for people believed that hard work deserved a reward, no matter the worker's mental equipment. Say what you would, that Dippy was a sure-enough hustler.

What they didn't know—the older ones who bought his glass cutters and extracts—was that Dippy's stock included pictures and picture magazines that he drooled over as he showed them secretly to drooling teen-agers. Dippy didn't smoke, drink, gamble or even swear, people said, ignorant of Dippy's devotion to the remaining pursuit.

"A man's got to keep up with the times, kid," he told me when I met him in front of the bank, which, like most places in town, had closed down for the funeral. Because he spit a fine spray when making his spiel, I took a step back. "Christ, yes, he does," Dippy went on. "Things changin' everywhere every day."

I allowed that was true.

"Any magazine you want, I can subscribe you to it. Cheap, too. And papers, big-city papers, from Chicago to Spokane. Yes, sir, a man's got to keep up with the times."

"Yeah," I answered. "So why didn't you hear about Buster Hogue's funeral?"

Dippy scratched his head and looked up and down the empty street. "So that's it," he said. "He bought some stuff from me onct. And they're layin' him away, eh?"

"It seemed best. He's dead."

"Sure, I see," Dippy answered. "Bad day for me, then. But there'll be some folks stayin' home. Now, kid, maybe you ain't interested yet in current events, but you sure God will perk up when I show you some pictures I got and some samples of magazines. Pictures like you never seen. Women and men, havin' their fun. Me'n' you will go off somewheres private and have a look."

Somehow Geet Hawthorne came to my mind, and I felt unworthy, and I answered, "No, dammit! Keep your damn dirty pictures."

I left him looking puzzled but undefeated. After all, everybody had to keep up with the times, public and private.

I kept up with the times by going to the post office, looking in our empty box and lazing on home. I worked then on my Buster Hogue murder report, which I had sneaked out of the office, and had a fidgety go at *The Moonstone*, which the sheriff had lent me.

It struck me, after I had read twenty-five pages or so, that maybe old Mrs. Jenkins wanted another chicken dispatched for the pot. Probably she hadn't gone to the funeral, and it wouldn't hurt to ask the old girl.

Dippy Ferguson was there before me, and I paused outside the picket fence, seeing that Mrs. Jenkins already had opened the door. I couldn't quite hear what was being said until Mrs. Jenkins lifted her cracked voice in song. Then I could hear all right. So could anybody if he'd happened to be within crow call.

What she sang was her answer, off-key to some tune that had popped into her head. "No, I don't want your paper."

Dippy was equal to the occasion. To a melody of his own, faster in beat than her bit, he sang back, "Oh, yes, you want to know the news." He sang a pretty fair tenor, though, I imagined, quite spitty.

That opened the ball, or should I say opera?

Delighted at the presence of a fellow singer, Mrs. Jenkins put more spirit into her next selection.

Pass the good, pass the good,
With a will, with a will,
Just a word or smile or song.
Be it ever so small
Don't keep it all.
Just pass the good along.

I could guess what construction Dippy would put on that sentiment, and he didn't disappoint me. In stronger voice, to the tune of "In the Good Old Summertime," he answered, gesturing appropriately:

The boy he climbed the fire escape
And got there just in time
To see her tootsie-wootsie
In the good old summertime.

Mrs. Jenkins disappeared inside. When she came back, she had an old horse pistol in her hand, which shook with the weight of it. The pistol went off, and so did Dippy. He cleared the gate near me by about five feet and was gone like an antelope, leaving as spoor a scattering of papers.

I gave Mrs. Jenkins what I thought was time

enough to cool off, but when I knocked at the door and it opened, she still held the pistol.

"Mrs. Jenkins," I said. "It's just me. Jase. You know. Jason Beard."

There wasn't a flicker of recognition in the old face. She appeared ready to fire that cannon again. She said, "Lay not wait, O wicked man, against the dwelling of the righteous."

In its wanderings the cannon kept picking me up, and I ducked and ran.

The sheriff had returned from the graveyard. I told him my story, all of it, as fast as I could. He had to laugh, but his laugh was rueful, and he got right to business. "Jimmy," he called, and Jimmy appeared. "Your wife working?"

"Not now. Last patient got well."

"Tell her I'll need her, beginning tonight."

Charleston and I got in the Special and drove to Mrs. Jenkins' house. He knocked at the door.

Mrs. Jenkins answered the knock, all smiles. "Well, Sheriff Charleston and Jase. Come in, both of you."

As soon as we entered, I smelled something burning and without asking leave hurried to the kitchen. A pot had boiled dry. Whatever had been in it was crust now, and the pot was ready to melt. I found a hot pad, put the pot in the sink and turned off the gas.

"You'll have to excuse me, Mrs. Jenkins," I said on returning. "A pot had burned dry. I turned off the gas."

"Oh, did you?" she answered.

Charleston spoke in his blandest voice. "I understand, Mrs. Jenkins, that a man has been molesting you."

"Was he?" The old eyes looked at Charleston for confirmation. "I guess so, then."

"So tonight—and I hope you agree—I want Mrs. Jimmy Conner to be here. She knows how to deal with bad actors."

"I see," she answered. "I suppose there's no one in the spare room, last I heard, anyway."

"You can put Mrs. Conner up, then?"

"Why, I imagine. Mr. Jenkins is away, you know."

"Yes, I know. Thank you. I'll be back later with Mrs. Conner."

I spotted the pistol at the same time the sheriff did. It lay, plain enough, on a chest in the hall. The sheriff was ahead of me on the way out, and Mrs. Jenkins behind, and I screened him from her sight for the moment it took him to push the thing in his pocket.

There were no laughs in either of us as we drove back to the office. All Charleston said was, "Jase, old age is a cruel thing. It lays waste body and mind, one or the other or both. 'The last of life for which the first was made.' Shit!"

CHAPTER ELEVEN

Except that the time was morning and the date nine days later, the scene was something like the opener, for charging into the office came Loose Lip Lancaster, mouth open, to report a murder.

I had been sitting in the sheriff's office, listening to him on the phone as he made arrangements for an incompetency hearing for old Mrs. Jenkins. District Judge Hiram Todd wasn't holding court at the time, either in our town or elsewhere in his jurisdiction and was reluctant, I gathered, to schedule a hearing.

"I'm damn sorry, too Judge," Charleston was saying, "but the county can't act or afford to act as permanent custodian."

Judge Todd, I knew, wasn't balking from laziness. He just hated the prospect. A soft-spoken man, not so lately from Kentucky, he had too much tolerance to be on the bench. Which accounted for his poor record on reversals by the Court of Appeals and his long popularity with the voters.

"I know, Judge," Charleston answered to another objection. "I know she's a fine woman—or was. But the fact is she can't be left to live alone any longer. What? You don't have to ask me that. Of course she doesn't have enough money to employ someone to watch out for her, even were someone available." After a pause, the sheriff said, "Thank you, Judge Todd. Four o'clock today," and it was right then that Lancaster barged in.

"Be goddam, Sheriff!" he was crying as he opened the door. "Be goddam, another killin' on top of one you ain't solved!"

"Slow down, Loose. Who?"

"Ben Day. That's who. Shot dead. I seen him." Lancaster perched on the edge of a chair like a bird about to take off. "We got a crime wave."

"Where? When?" The sheriff, now standing, rapped out the questions.

"On his own place, maybe two hundred yards from his mailbox. When? I seen him when I was comin' in. There was kind of a low-lyin' fog, and me, on my way to town, thought it was a downed critter at first. So I pulled up and went for a look. Deader'n hell. Ask anybody."

"Who else? You tell his wife? Does she know?"

"Tell her? Christ, no. You think I was goin' to the house and blab out, 'Sorry, ma'am, but your man has been kilt'?"

"Couldn't she see him?"

"Nope. The house, you'll recollect, sets maybe half a mile from the road where the mailbox is at. There's a hump, a knoll, between house and box, and he was lyin' yon side of it from the house. Coughed his life blood out all around. Anyone but me might not have spotted him on account of the fog."

"You're a genius," Charleston said. "All right. You'll ride with me. I'll rout out Felix Underwood first." He took hold of the phone. "Jase, round up Old Doc Yak and drive out with him."

"What you want with a doctor?" Lancaster broke in. "I done told you he's dead."

Charleston lifted the receiver. "So was Buster Hogue according to you."

Before he got his number, Charleston shouted, "Halvor! Halvor!"

Halvor showed up from the back, where he had probably been playing pinochle with a drying-up drunk who had the run of the jail.

"Felix," Charleston said to the phone. "Hold on a minute. Halvor, take charge here! Jase, move! Now Felix . . ."

It wasn't always easy to find Old Doc Yak. I went from his office to the Commercial Cafe to the Bar Star, asking questions, and then from one patient to a second. I found him in one of Duke Appleby's bedrooms, where he was prescribing pills for one of Appleby's kids who had tonsillitis. He shed his bedside manner when I told him the news.

Riding with Doc Yak was like sledding hell-bent through a field of boulders. While on the highway we got along fairly well, though the doc seemed to think the center line was put there to straddle—which annoyed a couple of tourists who took to the ditch. But once off the pavement we bounced, thumped and careened. I doubt that Doc Yak missed one promising rock. At any rate I gave him a grade of 90 per cent, which amounted to a solid A in assault.

The old automobile answered to the punishment with rattles, thumps and groans but somehow held together, and, no doubt in appreciation, Doc Yak said, loud above the clatter. "One thing about old machines, they have good stuff in them."

"Bound to," I answered.

"Yep," he went on as the right rear wheel churned its way up and out of a soft shoulder, "and they hang to the road, these old cars do."

I said I was glad and I was, for the shoulder overhung a ten-foot-deep borrow pit. I had thought we were going to roll there and have to be taken out, mangled, with torches.

There was one speed for Doc Yak on the open road, and that was full throttle—too fast if a cylinder or two hadn't been missing. Even so, we made time. In spite of our late start I could see dust rising at two points ahead of us and knew Felix and the sheriff weren't too far in advance.

Doc wheeled into the lane to the scratch of gravel and the squeal of tires and, bag in hand, jumped out of the car before it quit moving. I yanked the brake on.

Charleston and Felix Underwood and Lancaster and Bodie Dunn, who helped Felix occasionally, were standing and looking down at what was left of Ben Day. The Special was parked close by and so was the hearse, its end opened and left waiting for stuffing like a dressed turkey.

"Didn't I tell you?" Lancaster was saying. "Think I'm so dumb I can't tell a goner?"

I edged up while Doc bent to examine the body. They say some people look better dead than alive. Ben Day didn't. It was as if death had peeled off any mark of civility, leaving just orneriness. There was blood on his chin and some on his hands and a sopping of blood on his work shirt. He had on an open leather jacket, faded jeans and tennis shoes and wore a holstered and belted six-shooter.

Doc laid open the jacket and shirt and skinned up the undershirt so's to look at the chest. There was what looked like a bullet hole rather low on the right side but no blood to speak of. Doc fumbled in his bag, extracted his stethoscope as if out of habit and pitched it back in to the shake of his head. "Any fool can see he's dead," he said. "Dead some time."

"How long, Doc?" Charleston asked.

"God knows. Or the devil. Six, eight hours at a guess. Midnight maybe. I'm no laboratory, you know."

The sheriff said, "Thanks."

Doc turned the body over and peeled up the clothes. "The bullet's still in him. No mark of exit."

Charleston nodded, saying, "So?"

"See for yourself."

"I do."

"Lung punctured and maybe the liver," Doc Yak

went on. "That's a guess again. No use making sure here and now."

Charleston said, "Felix, you want to break the news to Mrs. Day?"

"You'd think, by God, she'd have showed up. What does it take, a circus parade? Not that I mind, though."

I figured Felix didn't. He was used to that kind of thing and could shed tears of sympathy while selling a thousand-dollar casket.

"Tell her I'll want to see her," Charleston said as Felix set out.

Doc Yak fastened his bag and stood up. "That's all for me now, I suppose."

"Stick around if you can," Charleston told him. "Maybe Mrs. Day or someone will want a ride into town. Maybe Jase, but I'd rather he didn't leave now."

Doc Yak gave an all-right, and the sheriff stooped over and went through Day's pockets. They didn't yield anything except matches and cigarettes. He examined the revolver and found it full loaded.

Charleston began nosing back toward the mailbox. There were splotches of blood here and there, and here and there tennis-shoe footprints between the tire tracks. He examined them as we went along and after a while said, "This is the way he came back from the mailbox, not the way he went to it."

I had been too dumb to mark that the footprints all pointed one way, toward the house in the rear of us.

The tin mailbox was open. Around it were drippings of blood and a place where the grass had been flattened as if a deer had lain there. "Here's where he got it," the sheriff said. "Knocked him down, bullet or shock, and it was a time before he could get to his feet. Tough man, Jase."

He looked in the mailbox. It was empty. The road was bordered here by low growth—buckbrush, white sweet clover, and the drooping stems of wild gaillardias and sunflowers. In it, maybe forty feet or less from the box, we came on another place where a deer might have lain.

But I knew, without being told, that a man with a

gun had screened himself there. We cast around for a shell casing without finding one. It was no wonder. An empty shell, ejected, could have nestled beyond sight in the growth.

Charleston went back to the box, studied the field near and far and struck out away from the graveled lane. I wasn't a tracker, as he obviously was, but I could make out now and then the marks of passage in the stiff, yellowed grass. The trail meandered, from ground swell to swell and from one clump of cinquefoil to another; and my imagination pictured Day, seeking cover in the starlight night on his way from the house to the box and all the same getting bushwhacked when he got there. Got there for what? And got it for what?

"I've seen enough," the sheriff said, and led the way back to the party.

Ben Day's body had been stuffed in the hearse and the end of the hearse closed up. Felix was talking to Mrs. Day. Behind her a piece, as if planted there by her order, were the Days' two ratty boys, ages eight and ten maybe.

"I think it best, Mrs. Day, if you don't view the body now," Felix was saying. "That's why I have moved it. Later"—he gave her a small professional wave—"of course."

Mrs. Day wasn't carrying on. She had the tired, washed look of a woman to whom everything had happened, so what was another item? She replied to Felix, "That's good enough."

"I'm sorry, Mrs. Day," the sheriff broke in, "but I hope you will feel like answering a few questions."

She answered, "I don't know nothin'."

"Did you know your husband left the house last night or early this morning? Did you hear him leave?"

"I don't pay no attention. He comes and he goes."

"And didn't you miss him this morning?"

She said the one word, "Him!" with such a bleak bitterness that I wished the sheriff wouldn't go on.

"Did you hear a shot or shots?"

"Someone always shootin' around here. If it ain't

jackrabbits it's deer, in season or out. I don't pay no attention."

"To your knowledge did anyone wish your husband dead?"

"To my knowledge, yes, sir. I can't count 'em."

"Not a particular one?"

"Buster Hogue, but I don't guess he took a gun to his grave."

The sheriff drew a deep breath. "It seems a little strange you didn't come down from the house earlier. You must have seen us drive in and pull up."

"I seen you. So what? I ain't curious like a cat."

"Do you mind if I come to the house, just to look at the guns your husband had?"

"Look all you want."

"Thank you. In the meantime Mr. Underwood will take the body to town."

"It ain't doin' no good here." In her words, in her tone she might have been saying he hadn't done any good, anytime, anywhere—not to her.

The others had stood around listening. Now Felix and Bodie Dunn started for the hearse. The sheriff took me aside a step or so. "You want to ride back with Doc Yak?"

"Not unless you want me dead in the hearse alongside Ben Day."

He gave his small, knowing smile. "I'll have Loose Lip ride with Doc. The trip will add to his repertoire."

And so it was arranged.

We trailed up to the house with Mrs. Day and her brats and made a quick search of the place. Apparently the only firearms Day had, besides his revolver which Charleston kept, were a .22 repeater and an old .30-06, which was the gun for elk and bear. Neither had been fired in some time.

As we left, Charleston said, "Thank you, Mrs. Day, and my sympathy. I may want to talk to you later."

She nodded her life-weary head.

On the trip back to town with the sheriff I said, "It's damn funny."

"What's funny?"

"Loose Lancaster. How come he's Johnny-on-the-spot all the time? How come he knew Day died from a bullet?"

Charleston answered, "Genius," and was silent for a time. "Jase," he asked then, "some of it's pretty plain, isn't it? Tennis shoes included."

"Tennis shoes?"

"Sneakers, Jase, to back up other evidence."

It dodged in my mind as he spoke that I never had seen Day in anything other than cowpuncher boots.

Evidence or not, the sheriff wasn't satisfied. His face as he drove had a look of troubled preoccupation, the weather lines etched at the sides of his mouth. "I don't know what I could have done, but I should have foreseen this."

"Foreseen what?"

"Day's getting shot. Damn it, a man who can't spot a pair in an open hand has no business in the game."

CHAPTER TWELVE

Felix with his telltale hearse and Doc Yak with his mouthy passenger were sure to have alerted the town before Charleston and I arrived. The time was early afternoon, and the weather was hotter than the pistol the sheriff didn't carry. He wasn't as faithful to his firearm as I was to my baseball.

"We can find out who did it just by listenin', Jase," Charleston said as we approached the fringe of the town.

I answered, "Oh?"

"Yeah." His teeth shone white as he glanced at me with a smile that had little fun in it. "Jesus save me! Comin' to the office will be more than three wise men who've seen the star. More'n that where men drink or feed. And those that see not will want me to tell 'em what isn't plain to my eye. We could run out to the graveyard and have some peace, I reckon, but no nourishment with it."

"Why not go to my house?" I asked. "It will be quiet there, and my mom will scrape up something to eat."

"I wasn't hinting. Why for should she?"

"For one sure thing, she'll be anxious about me. She is if I don't report pretty often. And she's probably heard about the shooting to boot, making her anxiouser."

"Don't mention grub then. All I want is to fight shy of my constituents for a spell."

I knew I wouldn't have to mention food, not to my mother.

We parked by the side of the house, where some old cottonwoods cast a shade while they dropped the last of their cotton.

I led the way to the back door and yelled, "Mother," though it turned out I didn't have to. She was in the kitchen.

"Jase," she said, "I'm so glad to see you, to know you're safe. Mabel Main called to tell me why and where you'd gone. It's so terrible. Oh, good afternoon, Mr. Charleston," she went on, catching sight of him hanging back from the doorway. "Please come in. It's so hot. I've made a pitcher of iced tea."

"I'm dodging my supporters, but I don't want to intrude," the sheriff answered, taking off his hat as men didn't according to him. It seemed to me that the edges of his hair had grown more silver in the last few days. Except that he was too thin of body and somewhat too young, he should have been in the Senate, where impressive older men guided the national destiny.

"Oh, bother your intrusion!" Mother said. "And I bet you're both hungry. I'll make sandwiches and bring in the tea. You two go in the living room. It's cooler there."

After we had sat down, I said, just to pass the

time, "The longer it goes on, the more suspects we have, it seems to me."

"And for sure the more bodies."

"That Mrs. Day now. She was awful indifferent. No grief at all."

The sheriff nodded, more as if in thought than in agreement with such suspicion. "I reckon she's had good cause to kill him many a time. Doesn't prove she did or didn't. And it doesn't connect."

"With Buster Hogue?"

"Right. Brooded by the same hen, I figure. But more suspects? Yeah, Jase. Or fewer."

We were quiet until Mother came in with iced tea, cold beef sandwiches and leftover lemon pie.

Charleston got up when she appeared. His good manners gave me a little pain, but not so with Mother.

She sat down with her sewing while we ate, but I could tell her mind wasn't on mending. Apparently Charleston could, too, for he said, "It was outright murder, Mrs. Beard. More than that we hardly know."

"And old Mrs. Jenkins?" she said in her gentle voice. "Jase told me. That will be a kind of putting to death, too, if she is committed."

"I dare to hope not," Charleston answered. His tone held regret but also a hard recognition of fact that came counter to Mother's softness. "It's possible she'll adjust happily to new circumstances. In any case we must act."

"It's cruel all the same."

"It's the years that are cruel, not society."

"But society, authority, will take what the years have left."

"Mrs. Beard"—the sheriff's voice had gone stern—"do you realize she might have killed your son yesterday?"

Mother's startled gaze fixed on me. "What? Killed you, Jase?"

"It's true," Charleston persisted. "She held a gun on him. Jase didn't tell you."

Mother asked, "Did she, son?"

They had made me uncomfortable, this man that I admired and the mother I loved, by coming so close to dispute. "She was just confused," I answered. "It was nothing to get you alarmed about. And the hearing is nothing, nothing, I mean, compared to two murders. Mr. Charleston should be free to center on them."

Charleston grinned briefly. "Ought to call me the jack-of-all-trades. Which reminds me. I must serve the citation on Mrs. Jenkins. The county attorney has prepared the petition."

We had finished eating, and he stood up. Before he thanked Mother, he carried his dishes into the kitchen. I followed suit, the example having been set. That act of the sheriff's was enough to melt any pique in my mother.

I was sure Charleston would go to the office after serving the citation on Mrs. Jenkins even if he had to listen to a lot of worthless theories about Day's murder, so I made some excuse to my mother and went to the courthouse after fiddling around for a while.

No one was in the office except Charleston and old Jimmy, who wasn't doing anything but drawing his pay. Charleston was on the phone, apparently waiting for someone to answer. He waved me toward the extension, saying, "I want you to be able to report to your mother that I tried."

"Doctor Pierpont," a voice said briskly.

"Good afternoon, Doctor Pierpont. Sheriff Charleston here. I'm glad I could find you."

"Yes?"

"I called on the bare chance you could help us. We have a hearing this afternoon, a case of senile incompetence—or insanity as the law has it—a hearing on a citation for commitment. I dislike to press it."

"Naturally."

"The defendant is, or has been, an excellent lady. I hate to see her carted off to the asylum, and I am wondering whether you could examine her and, perhaps, by your therapy, enable her to continue her life here. The county would pay you."

"How old is she?"

"I don't know. Seventy-odd, I would guess. Physically spry."

The doctor's voice was decisive. "It would be a waste of my time and the county's money, Sheriff."

"No possible help?"

"In a controlled environment, some help, some adjustment. Custodial help for the most part. There is little we can do about the problems of aging."

"I see. Thank you, Doctor. Oh, by the way, have you heard there's been another murder in the neighborhood of the canyon?"

"No! Who this time?"

"Day. Ben Day."

"Do I know him? Yes, I think, vaguely, by hearsay. And wasn't he at that wretched picnic?"

"He was. We found him dead inside his own field, not so far from his mailbox."

"And you're sure he was murdered?"

"No doubt about it on first examination."

"I don't envy you your job, Sheriff. No clues yet, I suppose. Two shootings and no clues."

"None worth a damn."

"Too bad. I can only wish you good luck."

"I'll need it. Thanks. But back to this case of senility. Nothing to do but stow her away, huh?"

"Right." He added, "Sorry."

Charleston said thanks again, hung up and turned to me. "Last gasp, and it turned out short and sweet. Don't forget to tell your mother, Jase."

As I was saying I wouldn't, the door opened and Guy Jamison came in, dressed like the dude's idea of the master of the outdoors. "Now I have maybe a little clue, Chick," he said.

The phone rang, and Charleston told Jimmy, "Get that damn phone in the other office, will you, Jim? Anything important, goose me. Go ahead, Guy."

"I was coming from the city last night with a car full of dudes. Late-ish. Going back today for some more. Anyhow, along about Ben Day's place I passed a strange car."

He waited until Charleston answered, "There's considerable traffic up there."

"Not at that hour, close to midnight. Now I can't

tell you just where. Day's land runs along the road for a mile, but there's a place on the road where the shoulder has given away, making a kind of tight squeeze. That's where we passed."

"Any idea of the make of the car, license number, driver?"

"It was too dark for a bat, Chick, and I had to watch the road so's not to hit him or fall in the ditch, and the dudes were jabbering, but I got the idea, the bare idea, the car wasn't local."

"Did you get a glimpse of the driver?"

"Glimpse is right. I wouldn't know him from the cue ball."

"But he wasn't a neighbor?"

"Hell, Chick, you ought to know a neighbor would have stopped, like I would've, and said good evening and how's tricks and all that. This man squeezed by, mum, and went on. I didn't give him or his car another thought until I heard about Ben Day an hour or so ago."

"All right, Guy." Charleston got up. "Maybe it will help. We're much obliged. Now Jase and I are due at court."

Jamison let himself out. The phone had rung a couple of times, and Charleston paused long enough to ask, raising his voice, "Anything important, Jimmy?"

Old Jimmy showed at the connecting door. "Yeah. Some joker says try a Ouija board."

The hearing for Mrs. Jenkins was held in the courtroom, not in chambers, but since it was special and the court not in regular session, no one but the involved parties attended, though once or twice the door to the room opened and someone peeked in only to leave. Judge Todd hadn't bothered to robe himself. Maybe he thought judicial appearance would rattle old Mrs. Jenkins.

Mrs Jenkins and Mrs. Conner sat in the second row of seats. Mrs. Conner, who was perhaps fifteen years younger than Jimmy, had dressed up for the occasion but still looked like a nurse, I thought guiltily, who could keep in fine fettle three or four babies.

The sheriff and I and Doc Yak occupied the first

row. Between us and the bench sat Marion Shannon, the court reporter, with his stenotype, and Montgomery Clough, the pip-squeak county attorney, who attended the hearing for reasons never apparent, since the judge himself took over the questioning.

The sheriff was the first witness. After he had been sworn and identified himself, Judge Todd said, "As you know, Sheriff Charleston, before the court is a petition to commit Mrs. Jennie Caine Jenkins."

I noticed he omitted the legal phrase, "for reasons of insanity." But it wouldn't have made any difference, I thought. Mrs. Jenkins sat as if lost and unhearing, her wrinkled hands held placid in her lap.

The judge was saying, "What can you tell the court, as a matter of fact, in support of the petition?"

"Not a great deal, myself," Charleston answered. "But it will be supported, Your Honor. And, of course, it is common knowledge that Mrs. Jenkins sings hymns, sings them aloud, on her daily march to the post office."

Judge Todd let a little smile crack the solemnity of his face. "You have heard of the First Amendment, Sheriff?"

"And defend it, Your Honor. It is her right to sing if she wants to. I point to it only as an oddity of behavior."

"Yes. Go on."

"Yesterday afternoon, Your Honor, Mr. Jason Beard came to my office to report that Mrs. Jenkins had taken a shot at a man and, later, threatened himself."

"The court will hear from Mr. Beard on that point."

"Yes. Then in company with Mr. Beard I called immediately at the home of Mrs. Jenkins."

"And?"

"She welcomed us."

"And seemed rational enough?"

"I can hardly say that. She was very vague, with no apparent memory of having shot at or threatened anybody. Also she seemed to think that her husband, dead now for a good many years, was away only temporarily."

By squirming around, I could steal another glance at Mrs. Jenkins. She sat without movement, unheeding, her eyes blank, clouded, lost somewhere in the long roll of her life. The years. They had left only scattered memories, the then time or times, and the rare, cruel grasp of the now.

I heard Judge Todd say, "That is the extent of your testimony?"

"Not quite, Your Honor," Charleston responded. "On the way out of the house I happened to see this revolver." The sheriff took it out of his pocket, which was insufficient to hide it, stood up and laid it on the bench. "It is an old forty-five with an eight-inch barrel, as you see, and it has been recently fired. Just once."

Judge Todd studied it, his eyes down-turned and tired. "Where?" he asked.

"On a chest or table just inside the entrance."

"The victim? The intended victim? Where is he?"

"Mr. Beard can tell you about him. We have been unable to locate him. I imagine he is a far piece away."

"Very well," Judge Todd said. "Stand down, Sheriff Charleston."

I was aware that Doc Yak, seated beside me, had been fidgeting throughout the proceedings. He was nervous by nature and in spite of his pills. Now, as the judge's eyes rested on me, Doc Yak stood up. "Your Honor," he said, "may I be heard? Necessarily I'm in a hurry."

"You are also in a court of law."

"Yes, Your Honor, but urgencies—"

"Sit down, Doctor. Before the court is an urgency, too, an important matter, a matter of a human life. And may I remind you that in a case of this kind the court and the medical profession act, so to speak, in concert? We must both hear the evidence. Then you may speak. Take the stand, Mr. Beard."

Doc Yak sat down as I went forward, but his head had a lift to it as if he might howl at the moon.

I went through the business of swearing and identifying myself.

"You're not a deputy in the sheriff's office?" Judge Todd asked, knowing very well I wasn't.

"No, Your Honor, I guess I'm just a hanger-on."

"But you help out when you can?"

I said I did.

"You were at the residence of Mrs. Jenkins yesterday afternoon?"

"Twice, sir. The first time I didn't go in because of that horse pistol there. The second time I did, along with Mr. Charleston."

"Tell the court about the first time."

"Well, Dippy Ferguson was there before me, and so I stopped by the fence."

"Can you identify the said Dippy Ferguson?"

"He was the man at the door. Oh, he's a door-to-door salesman of one thing and another, and he comes to town once in a while."

"And why were you there, outside Mrs. Jenkins' house?"

"To chop the head off a chicken, if she wanted me to."

The judge frowned, as if the reason demanded examination.

"I often did that for her," I told him, and added in the cause of justice, "for twenty-five cents."

"She paid you always?"

"She certainly did, Your Honor. Sometimes she got mixed up with the change, but I always straightened it out."

"I see. Go on. A man had preceded you?"

"Yes. Dippy Ferguson was at the door, trying to sell a magazine or newspaper subscription, as I got it, and Mrs. Jenkins sang out—I mean she really sang— 'No, I don't want your paper.'"

"And then?"

"Well, Dippy likes to sing, too, and he has a pretty good voice only he spits, and he didn't get the name Dippy for nothing, so he sang back to her that she needed to know the news. Then they had a kind of a song fest, not a duet but, I guess, opera style, singing back and forth. I stood and listened."

"These are facts?" Judge Todd asked, scratching his head. "Facts?"

"Yes, Your Honor. All facts."

"Tell the court more."

"She sang part of a hymn then, one you probably know. It tells you to pass the good around."

"And this Dippy person answered?"

"He sure did, but not what a man would expect if he didn't know Dippy. I suppose that line about passing the good set him off in his own way, like it would. His answer was a little off-color."

"Can you remember it?"

I could easy enough. It had been running through my head as things will, but I asked, "Must I, Judge?"

"If you please."

So, feeling foolish, I half sang "In the Good Old Summertime" with the tootsie-wootsie twist. Doing so, I looked at Mrs. Jenkins, wondering if she'd take a shot at me if she had a pistol. She wouldn't this time. Tootsie-wootsie passed her by.

Judge Todd had his hand over his face. Through it he said, "Read on, Jason."

"Mrs. Jenkins didn't like it, or it seems so, anyhow, because she backed into the house and came back with that old pistol and fired at Dippy."

"But missed him?"

"He didn't cripple away."

"Just the one shot?"

"That's all she had time for."

"Then what?"

"I thought I had given her time to cool off, but when I knocked at the door, she met me with that same revolver. I don't think she recognized me. She said evil had no business waiting on the homes of the righteous, or words to that effect. I can repeat her exactly if you give me a minute to think."

"Never mind. Did you try to reason with her?"

"Not very long. Would you, Judge?"

The judge passed his hand over his face again. Looking down from the witness box during my testimony, I had seen smiles, slow smiles, almost guilty, on the faces of the sheriff, Doc Yak and Mrs. Conner; and it came to me, earlier than to most, that humor and pathos were close kin. What's funny unless grounded in hurt?

"Do not address such questions to the court," the judge was telling me through his fingers.

"Sorry, Your Honor."

"Now on your second visit?"

"Mr. Charleston has told you about that—all but one thing."

"And that was?"

"When we showed up, I smelled smoke and beat it to the kitchen. A pot had boiled dry. It was red hot, and the burner was still on high. I attended to that and got to thinking that someday Mrs. Jenkins would burn the house down and herself along with it. She passed it off like it was nothing when I told her about it."

"Have you anything further?" Judge Todd asked.

"Nothing," I said and looked at old Mrs. Jenkins sitting there patiently. "Nothing, except it's a shame, a damn shame—"

"I know," the judge broke in. "Step down, Jason. Now, Doctor."

Doc Yak, moving like a bundle of hurried sticks, came forward and sat. I was reminded, during the swearing in, that he was really Gaylord Summerville, M.D.

"You do know Mrs. Jenkins, the defendant, Doctor?" Judge Todd asked.

"For forty years. Splendid woman. When she's at herself. Husband was my patient, too. Dead of cancer."

Doc Yak was rattling off answers as if, unless he hurried, some patient would perish of mere waiting.

"Your present opinion, Doctor, based on the evidence and your experience with her?"

Doc Yak wasn't looking at Mrs. Jenkins or she at him. He said, "I'm not forced to testify. Breach of professional ethics."

"But you will help the court, Doctor? You'll advise?"

"With reluctance. For her sake. Mrs. Jenkins calls me once or twice a week. Often I answer in person. Last time I made a house call—"

"When?"

Doc Yak took a worn little book from his hip pocket

and consulted it. "Three o'clock this past Wednesday, July twenty-three."

"Yes."

"She had forgotten she called me. Thought I was the plumber. Couldn't tell me what to plumb."

Behind me I heard Mrs. Jenkins tell Mrs. Conner, "Faucets. He knows very well it was leaky faucets."

Judge Todd rapped softly with his gavel. He could have heard the sounds but not the words. "So, Doctor? A diagnosis? Your opinion for the guidance of the court?"

"Senile dementia," Doc Yak answered as if the words were sour on his tongue. "Brain starved for blood. Nothing to do but commit her. I'm sorry."

"Thank you, Doctor. You may be excused."

Doc Yak clattered out of the witness box and galloped away.

Judge Todd said, "You have heard the evidence, Mrs. Jenkins. You are not represented by counsel, I see, nor is there any need of that in the eyes of this court. The question is: Do you wish to take the stand? Do you wish to appear in your own defense? Mrs. Jenkins? Do you hear me? Do you want to be heard?"

"Thank you," Mrs. Jenkins said, coming jerkily to her feet. Her eyes had gone away again, away from the faucets and plumber, into some cataract dimness of dream. "I have enjoyed myself, but I must go now. I have a guest." She stared around for the guest and found her at last in the person of Mrs. Conner, who had been holding her arm all the time. They left the courtroom.

"Sheriff," Judge Todd said then, "this has been a most irregular proceeding, but it is in accordance with the court's good judgment, if against its sentiments, that an emergency commitment in this case be issued at once. Central State Hospital has facilities, experts in mental disorders, that we lack here, and it can pass on her competency, insanity if you will, with an authority we don't possess. Court's adjourned."

Once inside his office the sheriff got rid of Halvor by asking if he wouldn't go buy some cigars. The girl clerk at the drugstore was a looker, and Halvor strode off. Then Charleston told me, "Jase, you're elected."

"To what, Mr. Charleston?"

"To driving Mrs. Jenkins, along with Mrs. Conner as her attendant, to Central State Hospital. Start early in the morning but take it easy—two days at least— because of Mrs. Jenkins' age and condition."

At the expression on my face he went on, "You know I can't go, not with two murders, last one just today. My outside deputy has his hands full there in the oil country. I wouldn't trust Jimmy to drive so far." He gave me a small smile. "And I wouldn't trust Halvor with Mrs. Conner, good woman as she may be. He might die of mammary smother. That leaves you. I'll fix you and Mrs. Conner up with official letters."

"But there's a ball game Sunday."

"Yes, Jase," he answered. "There's a ball game."

A silence hung between us.

I got up and said, "Please don't solve the murders while I'm gone."

CHAPTER THIRTEEN

The car I was to drive was a two-year-old Chev, assigned to the sheriff's office and used mostly by Halvor, since Jimmy didn't wheel around much and Charleston preferred his own Special. It could almost have passed for new. Charleston saw to that.

Before I left to pick up my passengers, the sheriff gave me a letter in witness of my responsibility and official mission and with it thirty dollars for expenses. Also, he handed over an envelope for Mrs. Conner. It contained, he told me, the commitment papers and a statement identifying the bearer.

Two suitcases and an overnight bag were waiting on Mrs. Jenkins' front porch. I stowed them in the trunk before knocking. Mrs. Conner, looking efficient though bulgy, answered the door. She carried a piece of hand luggage big enough for all Woolworth's cosmetics. Her other hand pulled Mrs. Jenkins along. Though her stockings didn't match, Mrs. Jenkins was dressed for the ball, the result of joint effort, no doubt.

Mrs. Conner locked the door, saying as she did so, "We'll have a nice ride, Mrs. Jenkins, and people will be so glad to see us. A beautiful day for an outing."

Mrs. Jenkins hung back. "I must be back before sundown. Where's my purse? Did you lock the door?"

"Yes. Yes. Everything's attended to. Here's your purse in my bag, if you'd rather carry it. Come on, now." Mrs. Conner managed to urge Mrs. Jenkins into the back seat, then climbed in herself.

It was a nice day all right. The sun, now perhaps two hours awake, shone gently—which was no promise it wouldn't blister us later—and the southwest wind was no more than a breath. What clouds there were were fluffy.

East of town, once we were out of the valley and up on the bench, the treeless land flowed away, so level and long it might have been planed by John Bunyan's carpenter. It was checkered by wheat fields that lapped and ebbed at the sides of the road, answering to the faint breeze. In a week or so would come harvest time. Here and there, rarely, was a house or a shack, forsaken now because wheat ranchers all lived in town so's to enjoy daily mail and flush toilets. Scattered cattle grazed or dozed in fields not touched by plows. The wild sweet clover that crowded the pavement gave off a scent. A dust devil played in a patch of summer fallow. I tooled the car toward the end of this flat world, toward the end of the world.

The two in back were silent, or spoke too low for my ears, until Mrs. Jenkins began to sing in her old, believing voice

Still He comforts mourning hearts,
Life and joy and peace imparts.

*   *   *

She was to sing that couplet, off and on, until
we pulled up for the night. When pauses came,
Mrs. Conner would say, "Yes, dear. That's sweet,
dear."

After a couple of hours the sun went into business.
It invaded the car like a torch, piercing the metal top,
blowing in through the air vents and then lying still
inside our enclosure like the spent breath of fever. To
open a window was to receive a blast.

I thought about the miles to Central State Hospital, which was called central because it was so far off
center. My mind went to Geet Hawthorne, standing
slim, cool and golden in her shaded retreat. Were her
eyes, was her face, on low beam or high? And then—
such are the wide swings of thought—I figured I'd
better watch for a gasoline station. Old people had
bladder trouble, and, come to think of it, I could use a
short leak myself. But when I slowed at sight of a
wayside truck stop, Mrs. Jenkins said, "You're poking,
Jase. I'll never get back." So I drove on, knowing I
could hold it as long as the next man and rating Mrs.
Jenkins as a good traveler.

An hour later I did stop, at a station in a burning
burg called Titus. Mrs. Conner saw her charge to the
ladies' room. After I had relieved myself, I bought
three cans of pop, courtesy of the sheriff's office, and
waited for my passengers. It wasn't much help, in that
heat, to remind myself that women always took an awful
time in the powder room. Was it because they didn't
have flexible spouts?

Mrs. Jenkins didn't look refreshed when she and
Mrs. Conner came out. She looked worn and removed,
as if the present had been washed out of her mind and
only the dim shores of remembrance remained.

I opened the pop cans and passed them around
and got the car under way. To my surprise Mrs. Conner
reached into her oversized bag and lifted out sandwiches.
They were fresh and well-flavored, made of homebaked
bread, and it struck me that old Jimmy had a pretty
good thing in his wife.

After two hundred miles Mrs. Conner said, "I think we've had enough for today, Jase. Don't you, Mrs. Jenkins?" She had to repeat her question.

Mrs. Jenkins answered, "Oh. What's that? Do we get out? Where's my purse?"

"It's in your hand, Mrs. Jenkins."

Mrs. Jenkins looked at her hand to make sure, said, "Oh," and asked, "What are we doing here?"

"Now don't you worry."

We were on the edge of Munroe, a fair-sized town, and here was a motel and a sign that read EATS. I pulled up and made arrangements for the night.

Mrs. Conner told me, "I think Mrs. Jenkins ought to rest for a while. Then we'll have supper."

"This isn't home," Mrs. Jenkins said as her faded eyes looked around. "Where are we? Oh, yes"—her gaze had come to her hand—"I've found my purse."

Mrs. Conner told her again not to worry.

I carried a couple of bags to their double room, saw the ladies inside and went back into the lobby, wondering how to pass the time. That question was solved for me. On TV was a baseball game, Giants versus Dodgers with Perry and Osteen pitching. I wished I had brought my baseball along.

The ladies showed up along about half-past five, and we went into the cafe. The special was pot roast, which was special because the menu said so. I washed it down with a chocolate shake, thinking good riddance. Before we started eating, Mrs. Jenkins fixed her misty eyes on me and said, "Ask the blessing."

I felt like a fool, there among strangers, but I muttered the bobtailed grace that my father used when under pressure.

Through with the meal, the ladies went at once to their room. I did, too, after tarrying long enough to buy a two-day-old Spokane paper for the sports news.

Just before we parted, Mrs. Conner had asked, "What time in the morning, Jase?"

"Six o'clock, I'd say. A hundred miles to go. With a good start we can make the return run tomorrow."

Mrs. Jenkins said, "Now. Please. I want to go back. You see—"

"You need a good night's rest," Mrs. Conner told her. "Don't you worry, dear."

They left me then, the early start being agreed on.

We arrived at the hospital about 9:30 the next morning. The drive was made without incident or much conversation except that Mrs. Jenkins had turned over the record, which nevertheless stuck again. She kept singing, sometimes low, sometimes high-quavering,

> *God will take care of you,*
> *O'er all the way,*
> *Through every day.*

I hoped to God He would though He hadn't.

The hospital consisted of a bunch of buildings, all old, some trees and ragged lawns on which a few people were lazing. They were the ones, I supposed, who had the run of the grounds because they didn't know where else to run.

I pulled up in front of a building marked ADMISSIONS and let the ladies out. I took Mrs. Jenkins' bags to a desk and headed for the door we had come in, not wanting to witness this final act of commitment, not with Mrs. Jenkins looking so old and so lost. Even her voice had failed her. She just stood, someone waiting, someone not waiting, for nothing.

On the wall near the entrance was posted a roster of the hospital's medical men. M.D.'s followed the names that I noticed, but what took my attention was an item at the bottom of the list that read:

ULYSSES PIERPONT, M.D.
Consultant in Psychiatry

A man stood outside the door, looking official while his eyes roamed over the privileged prisoners. I took him to be a guard and asked, just to make talk, "Doctor Pierpont here today?"

"Once a week. He flies in, usually on Wednesday,"

he answered, sizing me up to see whether I was a candidate for his jurisdiction. "You a friend of his?"

"I know him."

"A good man," he went on, having passed on my sanity. Then he added, as if glad to have someone of sound mind to talk to, "These other doctors, they're high muckymucks, too high for the likes of us poor personnel unless we got a chugged gut, but Doctor Pierpont now, don't think he's not all business but he's always got a friendly howdy for us and more'n that if the looney load ain't too heavy. He's a brain man, you know, what some call a head-shrinker or a skull-tinker. No matter of that, by God, he's good. More, like I say, not like his brother snot noses, he's always friendly to us. Treats us like humans."

"I would think so."

"Which makes him not too goddam popular with what you would call his colleagues. But he don't care. I guess the sons of bitches don't rate too high with him."

He stepped away. "That's my opinion. Take it or leave it. Mum it or gab it. So long. Time for my coffee break."

I moseyed around after he left, trying to fight shy of the inmates, but perhaps five minutes later a man in a full suit, plus tie, tugged at my arm. He might have been one of the doctors. "Good morning," I said.

He answered, "Good morning," and his eyes studied me. Then, abruptly, he whipped out and open the right side of his suit coat and announced, "Hart, Schaffner and Marx."

"I see," I said and beat it away from him. I could talk to old people in a way but to nuts, no way. I made for ADMISSIONS and the comfort of sanity mixed with senility.

Mrs. Conner was about to take leave of her charge. "Now, Mrs. Jenkins," she was saying, "here's your purse, and there are your bags, and you'll be all right. I have to leave you for a while."

"I have to be back before dark."

"Yes. I know."

A woman in whites stood near them, ready to take

Mrs. Jenkins away, into the dark she had to avoid before
it came on.

The lady in whites said, with professional, pin-
prick sincerity, "You'll be very happy here, Mrs. Jenkins.
We're so happy to have you."

Mrs. Jenkins turned her gentle, beseeching, confused gaze on me. "Please tell Mr. Jenkins I've been
delayed."

I managed to answer, "Sure, Mrs. Jenkins," and in
weak inspiration added, "And I'll feed and water your
chickens."

Mrs. Conner said, "Here's your purse."

I drove safely enough, going home, but still wheeled. I
wanted to see the mountains, to get out of this flatland
that dipped just for a couple of drying-up streams and
then leveled off into forever. I wanted to put distance
between Mrs. Jenkins and me. And in my mind all
along had been the murders which, damn it, might
have been solved, might be solved any minute, with
me unaware and unrecognized. That was what death
did to you: it let things go on without your knowledge,
assistance or credit. Mrs. Conner, beside me, didn't
make talk.

We were five or six miles short of that scorched
town of Titus, and then it happened.

I was driving at about 70 mph, plenty fast for the
chuck-holed, single-lane road, when a car as long as a
Detroit dream squeezed by me, blatting, and cut in too
soon after overhauling the Chev. Braking, I saw my
front fender crumple. The Detroit dream, rubber screech-
ing, wavered and swerved to the right toward the ditch.
I hit its right fender with my right front. It slewed
around, reversed in direction, and hung on the road's
shoulder. At a stand-still, looking back, I saw it totter-
ing. Then, like a half-wakened horse that decides it can
snooze some more, it turned on its side in the borrow
pit.

It did have, if not a driver, someone who had been
at the wheel. He got a free door cocked open, climbed

up and out and, feet scratching for footholds, mounted the shoulder. He looked big.

After one shout Mrs. Conner had gone quiet. I opened my door, slid out and stepped toward the man. He was marching on me.

"By God," he said and kept marching. He was big all right, and he had a face like an open-faced pie, slightly scorched. Close up, he spoke again, his breath smelling like a crowded saloon. "Fine fix you got me in, punk."

Blood was in my head, and, for an answer, I belted him in the belly. The wind went out of him, and he bent over. Bent over, he limped to the side of the road and threw up.

He came back, unbent, said, "Good punch, kid," and caught my chin with a lick so sharp I went down. I scrambled up, still full of fight, but he took a backward step and stayed me with a lifted hand, open palm toward me. "That makes us even," he said. "Now we can negotiate."

"Negotiate, hell!"

From behind me Mrs. Conner said, "I'm a witness. Remember that. A witness to drunken driving."

"Now. Now. Easy," the man answered. "I'm not drunk."

He didn't look it or act it, aside from that crazy driving, though his breath still came out of a bottle.

His eyes lifted from mine and fixed themselves on something behind me. I didn't fall for that old trick. "Kid," he said, "trust me, will you? My fault and all, I own up. Leave it to me, please."

I turned to look then. A state-patrol car had parked behind us, and a patrolman was striding our way.

"Officer," the big man said, "I'm in the wrong, I admit. I'm the offender."

The patrolman's eyes examined the wreckage and returned to the big man. "Let me see your driver's license." The big man fumbled out a fat wallet, opened it and held it out at arm's length, obviously so the patrolman wouldn't get a sniff of his breath.

To me the patrolman said, "Yours."

Mrs. Conner edged in and interrupted. "It's a wonder you don't ask if anyone's hurt."

The patrolman's gaze was calm. "Is there? Doesn't appear so."

"No," Mrs. Conner answered, "but there would have been if it wasn't for this boy here, the way he drove when that fool—"

"I've said I'm guilty, ma'am. I say it to all of you. No hard feelings, I hope. You see, officer, I bought this Cadillac just yesterday, and I haven't got used to its length. After passing this young man, I cut in too quick, not realizing how long was my tail. Stupid but understandable."

The patrolman was examining my credentials. "Sheriff Charleston," he said. "Give him hello from Tom Stevenson."

I said I would.

"Reckless driving," the patrolman told the big man, "and not the minimum bond, not with so much property damage. It's a county car to boot."

"I'll pay, of course." The fat wallet made a wave.

The patrolman and I stepped out for a look at the Chev. The bumper had a leer to it, and both fenders were bashed in, but that seemed the extent of the damage.

"Try the starter," the law said.

I did. The car started.

Quietly the patrolman advised me, "We'll make it enough. Two hundred dollars."

The big man didn't object when the patrolman named the sum. He seemed glad. "I'll pay it to this young fellow right now," he answered, and two hundred dollars in bills came to my hand.

"Does that suit you?" the patrolman asked me.

"I guess so."

"I'll make the bond the minimum then. Twenty-five dollars."

The big man seemed happy to pay that, too.

"If you wish to appear in court—" the patrolman began.

"Never mind. Never mind. I won't."

"I can have a wrecker sent out," the patrolman said as he handed the big man his receipt. "Titus is just down the line."

"My car will run, I think, once I get the fenders pulled up off the tires," I said.

All of us, except Mrs. Conner, attended to that chore. The big man, on account of his breath, was careful not to heave side by side with the law.

The big man gave us a smile then, a good smile, a smile that would have charmed a dyspeptic. "If this young man will just give me a ride into Titus, I can attend to the wrecker. It appears he's not crowded."

The patrolman asked me, "What about it? It happens to be convenient to me."

"I guess so."

While the patrolman and I watched, the big man went confidently to his overturned car, gophered into it, and came out with a bag and a briefcase. I opened the trunk for them.

The patrolman tucked his book under his arm, strode to the state car and drove around us. As he passed, he slowed to tell the big man, "No funny business."

There wouldn't be any anyhow, I felt sure, but all the same it reassured me, when the big man ushered Mrs. Conner into the back seat, to see that she had a fist-sized rock in her hand. He got in with me, smiling.

"Do I get it," he said as we started to roll, "that you have something to do with the law?"

"Something."

"Good, but there's no future in it. I always say get into sales."

I thought of Dippy Ferguson and answered, "Some don't do so hot."

"Chicken-coop stuff. Door to door. Big deals I'm talking about. I've made fortunes for many a man and haven't done so bad for myself." Easy money seemed to drip from his mouth. "But that's not here or there. Where you bound, son?" I had graduated from punk.

"Midbury."

"Now that's a coincidence. Same here. Don't want to put you out, but how about taking me all the way?"

Because we had entered Titus and a garage just ahead advertised a wrecking service, I didn't ask, not then, what was his hurry. I just answered, "I guess so."

The big man went into the garage and talked for a couple of minutes. Mrs. Conner was cradling her rock, ready to reduce him to a patient. He came out and said, "All set," and resumed the seat beside me. "These hick nut-and-bolt boys know more than the big-time Jesse Jameses."

On the road again I did ask him, "What's your hurry?"

"Hurry," he said. "Yep. Hurry. That was the cause of our accident."

"You were damn slow to admit it."

He laughed what seemed an honest laugh. "My boy, a position, clearly stated and boldly maintained— that's the secret of success in law, politics, salesmanship and whatever."

"It wasn't working so well with me."

"Ah, but it might have. The patrolman messed me up." He chuckled, remembering. "I'm insured to the limit."

"You haven't told me yet what was your hurry and still is."

"Long story," he answered, breathing a boozy sigh. "You happen to know one Ben Day?"

"He's dead."

"So I heard yesterday. My name's Michael, Mike for short, Day. He's my brother."

"Sorry."

"My brother, and he owes me money to boot. I set him up in business, made the down payment on that ranch of his."

"Him?"

"Age of innocence," he answered as if his innocence was long gone. "Eight years ago, and, God rest his deadbeat soul, never a payment made and the note not renewed."

"Too late now, so what's the hurry?"

He was silent for a minute, perhaps debating how much to tell. "Big mix-up," he answered then. "That damn note—I got it in my pocket—the statute of limit⁀-tions ran out the very day he got croaked. You get the picture?"

"Part of it, anyhow."

"I'm putting in my claim quick. If only my damn brother had signed a renewal!"

"Maybe his will takes care of that."

"Will! Ben make a will? Nuts. There'll be an administrator appointed by court."

"That would be his wife, his widow, wouldn't it?"

"Ha," he said. "Sweet Marcy Belle." He leaned over and whispered in my ear, his breath still pretty rank, "She couldn't read 'shit' if it was spelled out in cow dabs."

"So?"

"That's it. So?"

He fell silent then, as if for his part the subject was ended. That suited me.

I wheeled the quiet miles, thinking of one thing and another, including crumpled fenders, a brother interested in money to the exclusion of murder and my report to the sheriff. Foxy was the name for the Days, foxy tough for the dead one, plain foxy for Mike. I thought about Mrs. Jenkins, murder, the Hawthornes, the ball game I'd missed and Mrs. Jenkins' chickens.

The sun had started its slant to the west, and the heat of it burned in the car. I blinked against the shine, driving steady except for a sandwich-and-drink stop. I could begin to see the mountains, shapes of blue mist straight ahead. We would be home, I figured, some-where around nine o'clock.

The miles went by, marked by the idle bits of talk, and a fire lit itself in the west, and by and by we dropped down from the bench to the valley, not soon enough, quite, to be home before dark.

"Just let me off anywhere," Mike Day said. "I'll make out."

I left him and his bag and his briefcase in front of the Jackson Hotel. Before he took leave, he thanked me

and Mrs. Conner warmly, though it would have taken
more than warm thanks to thaw her. Then I drove her
to her house and said my own thanks regardless that
she was on a per diem. She dropped her rock by the
sidewalk.

After I parked the beat-up car in the rear of the
courthouse, I made for the sheriff's office, from which
shone the only light in the building. Halvor was seated
in the sheriff's chair with his feet on the desk and his
hands on a picture magazine. He said, "Hello, Sherlock."

"Hello yourself. Know where I can find Mr.
Charleston?"

"Yep. Gone to the city. Gone to the city on business is what he said." Halvor grinned. "That's what he
said, but I just happened to notice, lookin' out the
window, that he had a dame with him."

"Who?"

"Search me, but she was a dish, a real honest-to-
God dish."

I left. I would report tomorrow, after feeding Mrs.
Jenkins' damn chickens.

CHAPTER FOURTEEN

It was noon the next day before I got up, a fact that I
blamed on my mother, who usually routed me out if I
slept through the alarm. She answered to my complaint
by saying a growing boy needed his sleep, especially
after a hard day, and a lamb chop and a couple of eggs
would promote health and soothe temper.

The mention of eggs was a reminder, so I asked her
to hold up while I saw to Mrs. Jenkins' chickens, which
were just a hop-skip away and probably weren't hop-

ping or skipping, times being so hard. At this noon hour the sheriff's office could wait.

The chickens were all right, or anyhow live enough to appreciate feed and water.

It was five minutes past one when I walked into the sheriff's office. Jimmy Conner motioned toward the little-used room that was private when the door was closed. "He's waitin'," he said, "and he's done seen the wreck you dragged in. Like a kid, you ran into a daydream, I reckon."

Instead of answering, I knocked at the door, and Charleston's voice told me to enter.

He wasn't alone. In one of the four chairs near the desk sat a stringy character he introduced as Gus Gewald, who greeted me shortly in a voice that put me in mind of a hacksaw on the push.

"Mr. Gewald is a state criminal investigator," Charleston said, "and he's here to help us unravel our mystery." He spoke in a tone of easy tolerance, which still had a barb in it like the point of a fishhook inside a worm. "How'd you make out yesterday, Jase?"

Gewald hitched back in his chair, impatient at interruption, I supposed.

"All right except for the car. Jimmy said you'd already seen it." I handed Charleston the two hundred dollars, saying, "Here's to pay for the wreck. I couldn't help—"

Charleston waved explanations away.

"And here's what's left of expense money," I went on and gave him ten dollars plus twenty cents. "I'll make out a report."

"In time, Jase. In time."

"So now can the two of us get back to work?" Gewald rasped out, hunching forward.

"The three of us," Charleston answered.

Gewald sized me up, or rather down, like a bartender wondering was I old enough for a beer. "Pretty much of a pup," he said, turning to Charleston.

"He's got a good nose," Charleston answered. "Besides, he's my pup."

"Have it your own way. It's not mine. Back to business, then."

"You have the full report," Charleston told him. "All that we know, Jase and I."

"But none of your theories. No suspicions. No hunches."

"I wouldn't want to mislead a state criminal investigator."

"You can cut out the sarcasm. I was sent here."

"Not by my request, Mr. Gewald."

"No. But you weren't getting anywhere, not anywhere. The attorney general thought it was time a trained man took a hand."

"Take it, then." The words were sharp but came out smooth. "Let us know when and if we can help."

"There are, you know, quite a number of possibilities," Gewald said, as if it were beyond our power to think of a one. His voice seemed to get softer the more he sawed with it. "Assume, for instance, that Buster Hogue, now dead, was rolling Mrs. Day on the sly."

"I got a very balky imagination there," Charleston answered.

"Nevertheless, assume it. Buster Hogue was a single man, a long-time widower, and stranger things happen."

Here, I thought to myself, the state criminal investigator had jumped the reservation and faded from sight. Buster Hogue had been fifty or more, older by perhaps fifteen years than Chick Charleston himself. And Mrs. Day? No—squared, trebled and multiplied to infinity.

"Take assignations for granted, take them for discovered," Gewald continued, "it would be in the nature of Ben Day, then, to murder Hogue. Right?"

"Maybe," Charleston replied. "He wasn't what you could call an ever-lovin' husband, though."

"But to proceed. If he did, and one of the Hogue boys knew or even suspected? Well, there you would be."

Charleston said, "Sure enough."

"All right. Unlikely. I'll switch to the Hogue brothers. It's altogether possible, as I see it, that that dumb one, Simp, pot shot his father."

Nodding, Charleston said, "Possible."

"The psychiatrist so stated, even if somewhat reluctantly. Then couldn't Simp have gone after Day, too?"

"Why?"

"I don't know. Old animosity stemming from that Forest Service mix-up. Threat of exposure perhaps. And if not Simp, what about Junior, his brother, who's so protective of him? Put it this way: Simp shoots his father, Day knows it or gets wind of it, one way or another Junior finds out that Day's wise to the fact and so shuts him up with a bullet. The big-brother act. Or it could be that Junior himself did away with both men, killing Day after shooting his father because Day knew too damn much."

"You sure run the scale. I don't know why either Hogue boy would shoot his old man."

"Simp could have some looney reason."

"Yep. And Junior inherits." Charleston was shaking his head slowly, saying no to himself more than to us. It has been bothersome."

"And still is." Gewald's stringy frame came forward with his words. "Look. I want to talk to those boys. I want to talk to that professor who says he had his gun stolen. I want to talk to everyone who had trouble with Hogue. Hell, there are motives all over the place, for one murder or the other and the two combined, no matter if there's one killer or two. And I want to talk to Mrs. Ben Day. By your report she took the news of Ben's death very cool. Her husband dead, and her like an oyster. That jells with the business of assignation. Right?"

"She might still be in town," Charleston told Gewald. "This morning she testified at the inquest you missed."

I put in, "Inquest? Already? What was brought out, Mr. Charleston?"

He gave me a half-smile with humor behind it, said, "Person or persons unknown," went to the door and, opening it, called out, "Jimmy! See if you can round up Mrs. Ben Day somewhere in town and ask her if she won't please come to the office."

While we waited I made my report of the trip. Gewald sat back, resting his hacksaw for other metal.

"Patrolman Tom Stevenson asked me to give you hello," I told Charleston. "Also he decided the wreck wasn't my fault."

"Not surprising to me, Jase. Now about this Mike Day?"

"He wants to get his claim in, like I said, and I bet he's aiming to get himself named administrator of Ben's estate."

"Another Day another dollar, huh? Where's he from?"

"He didn't say. Roundabout, I guess. I took note of his license number. Minnesota plates."

Now Gewald interrupted, his voice sharp again. "He's not known around here? Not seen by anybody?"

"Seen by me and Mrs. Conner," I answered, feeling I was in tune with the sheriff . "And probably his brother Ben knew him. He said he did."

To me he said, "Nuts," and to Charleston, "Are you and your boy through?" "Boy" meant punk.

"For now, I reckon."

"I've got wheels, of course, to take me around to these people, but I'll need someone with me who knows the lay of the land."

"Sure. No trouble."

"Right now it's only interrogations that hold any promise. The evidence is damn scanty—one spent cartridge casing and a flattened bullet dug out of a corpse that appears to be the same caliber. No casts of tire prints. No fingerprints. No nothing else."

"Nary thing, Mr. Gewald. Nary thing."

What Gewald might have said wasn't said because Jimmy knocked at the door and showed Mrs. Day in. With her, not to my lasting surprise, was Mike Day. He wore a dark business suit, as befitted grief, and a sunrise necktie, as didn't. Mrs. Day had on a black outfit that had been new once and maybe stylish. Her face was blank, as if troubles rubbed on troubles had erased all feeling. And yet it struck me, struck me for the first time, that decent clothes and an injection of cheer would make her a good-looking woman.

Standing behind his desk, Charleston introduced Mrs. Day to Gewald, who rose half out of his chair. "And you," he continued, "must be Mike Day. Jase has told me about you."

"Yes, sir," Day answered with his salesman's confidence. "We met, though under unfortunate circumstances, occasioned, I must admit, by yours truly. I have made ample restitution, I hope." He went on, "You know poor Ben is, or was, my brother. I thought—I hoped—that it would be quite all right with you if I accompanied Marcy Belle here."

"Sit down, you and Mrs. Day," Charleston said.

Gewald held them up. "You're not an attorney." The words were more charge than question.

"No, sir. Indeed not. Just a relative and friend. I might add, however, that in earlier years I served as police judge. Two terms. Naturally I know something of law."

Charleston got the two visitors to sit down. Gewald didn't look pleased. Seated himself, Charleston opened the wide drawer of his desk, fumbled around and came out with one of his special cigars, which he didn't light.

"Mrs. Day," Gewald said, easing off on his saw, "you know I am here as a representative of the state. We want to find out who killed your husband and hope to advance toward a solution by getting your answers to some questions. Of course, you want to know, too."

"May I intrude?" Mike Day asked, not really asking. "Marcy Belle, you don't have to answer any questions. You may stay mute. Under the law a suspect may not be forced to incriminate himself."

Now Gewald employed his saw. "Who says she's a suspect? This is informal. No notes. No reporter."

"Thank you, Mr. Gewald," Day said, his big pie face split in a smile. "I am sure, sir, that you merely overlooked the customary precautionary statements antecedent to interrogation. Not that Marcy Belle has anything to conceal. I was merely making sure, for your sake, that procedure be proper."

Looking at him, looking at that large, whiskey-blushed, four-flusher's face, I felt an uneasy surge of liking for him, a surge not lessened by Gewald's expression. He was putting on a show, Day was. He was showing up Gewald. And he wasn't hurting himself with Marcy Belle. Charleston was leaning back, by aspect satisfied.

"All right. All right," Gewald rasped. "Consider made the statements of your rights under the law, Mrs. Day. Now, to get down to business, it has been remarked that your reaction to your husband's murder was cool, was indifferent. That's putting it mildly. What do you have to say about that?"

"A loaded and leading question," Mike Day interrupted. "Answer him if you wish, Marcy Belle."

She asked, "What?"

Gewald tried again. "The inference is, from your attitude, that you and he were at odds and hence that his death left you undisturbed. Now I ask you what you held against him."

"Say it again."

"You held something against him, didn't you?"

"I wasn't there. I didn't hold nothin'."

"I don't mean anything physical, nothing that you could hold in your hand." Exasperation was putting a harder edge on the saw. "What did you hold against him in your mind?"

"What every woman does."

"Every woman? Every one of his women? Did he have so many then?"

"How would I know?"

Gewald sighed, but exasperation clawed his face. "Look. Try to answer me. You said every woman. What do you mean by that?"

"Every woman that's a wife, that's what I mean." The words came live from the blank face and for an instant stood before me like truth chiseled in stone.

"Oh, you are saying that the lot of the wife—all wives—is unequal and burdensome?"

"Is that what I said?"

Mike Day broke in, smiling wide. "Sir, can you couch your questions in simpler language? Mrs. Day doesn't comprehend your polysyllabicisms."

Gewald tightened his mouth, looking at no one. I figured he was counting syllables himself. Then he said, "So be it. Mrs. Day, did your husband abuse you, mistreat you, maltreat you?"

She looked at Mike Day, who translated, "Did he beat you up?"

"What if he did?"

"It would give you a motive for removing him from the scene."

"He removed hisself by hisself from the scene, night or day, work or not, it didn't matter. I didn't have nothin' to say about that. He just went."

Was there, I wondered, some sly, some native and hidden intelligence behind her answers. No one could be that dumb. Yes? No? She began to be the second person I didn't quite want to admire but still did.

Gewald, the trained man, representative of the state, looked as if the quality of patience had had the hell strained out of it.

"Down to cases," he said, sawing hard. "Did you kill your husband?"

"I'm glad you're not a suspect, Marcy Belle," Day put in pleasantly.

"Did you kill your husband?"

"Me? Kill him? Mister, I'm lucky to be here myself, havin' him for a husband."

"Did you kill him?"

"Not so's you could notice."

"Did you?"

"I said no. How many times I got to say it?"

Came a pause, and I glanced around. Mike Day sat back, his arms folded over his heavy chest, his appearance suggesting what I would call large satisfaction. Knowing Charleston so well, I could tell he was amused.

Gewald returned to the attack, using what I supposed he thought was soft persuasion. "All right, Mrs.

Day. Thank you. Now I must go on to a delicate subject."

She just looked at him, her mouth slack. I could see her tongue fiddling with her lower teeth, which were good barring a vacancy a fist might have left.

"You knew Buster Hogue?"

"Sure."

"How well did you know him?"

"Well enough, I guess."

"Well enough that your relations were intimate?"

"Even after him and Ben had their trouble, I always spoke to him nice and he answered nice."

"That's not what I'm trying to get at, and you know it. Assignations. Did you and he arrange assignations?"

She looked for help to Mike Day, who didn't help her unless his smile was a help.

"Assignations?" she asked.

"Yes. Assignations! Trysts! Lovers' meetings!" Gewald jerked to his feet and poked an outraged finger at her. "Goddammit, in plain words, woman, were you screwing him?"

"That's enough, Gewald," Charleston said in a voice not loud but carrying. His words didn't surprise me. They just made conscious my unconscious recognition that in him was a lot of the old western gentleman.

His order was wasted.

"Oh, screw!" Mrs. Day answered as if in sudden recognition. She began laughing, laughing a laugh that hit me as sad and low-order and yet somehow pitifully fetching. "Me and Mr. Buster Hogue screwing! You got a mind, man, you have. I never had a chance even if he'd ast me." She sobered abruptly, and the old look of no hope settled back on her face. "Me with kids and never off the place and not a dime for so much as a new rag. Screw you, too, mister."

Gewald was looking at the floor for more questions, if any.

"Speakin' of kids," Mrs. Day said, "I gotta see about mine. I left 'em with a friend, and they'll likely be raisin' hell now if not sooner."

She got up, not to Gewald's objection, and went to

the door. He didn't have the grace to thank her, much less to apologize. Mike Day followed her, ushered her out and, before closing the door, said to all, "Her innocence is surely evident to you gentlemen. That being settled, tell me, Sheriff Charleston, are the judge's chambers upstairs?"

Gewald sat for a minute or two after they'd left, then got up, said, "I'll nose around," and went out the door.

Charleston lighted the cigar he'd been holding so long. "Jase," he said, breathing smoke, "a man ought to have to ante up for a show like we've seen."

"I kind of like that Mike Day, and Mrs. Day was great in her part."

He smiled and answered, "Sure. Good cast. Confidence man and the poor moron."

"And Gewald?"

"The trained investigator." He blew out a plume of smoke and added, "Trained in a crocodile school, I reckon."

"All bite and no brains, huh?"

"No, no, Jase. But bite before brains." He started to get up.

"Unless you have something else for me," I told him, "I'll get on with my written report, you know, about the whole case. But gee, Mr. Charleston, I can't remember everything that was said here."

He chuckled then. "Don't have to." He opened the big drawer of his desk and brought out a thing wrapped in a towel. "The towel's a silencer," he said as he unwrapped it. "But see, Jase."

Inside the towel was a cassette recorder and just outside it, so's to pick up the voices, a little microphone.

I gawked. "And you turned it on when you fingered around for that cigar?"

"Good thinking, boy."

"Thank you. Thank you a lot."

"Not too much, Jase. Remember, I'm just a sheriff, and Gewald represents the state and belongs to the opposition party to boot. So it wasn't just for your sake."

CHAPTER FIFTEEN

I arrived at the sheriff's office next morning just as Charleston did. We went in together and sat. He pushed to the side of his desk a clutter of accumulated paper, his manner indicating he couldn't be bothered with such trifles now, if indeed, ever. Halvor had given us good-morning and taken a newspaper into the private room where he could read without being interrupted by current events.

"No Gewald yet?" I said.

"Not until first thing this afternoon," he answered. "He's scratching around some more first."

"Where?"

"Old holes not worth scratching at. I had the pisswillie luck to meet him at breakfast. He said he wanted to talk to Felix Underwood and Doc Yak and other assorted characters who might hold a clue unbeknownst."

"Fat chance."

"Jase," he asked, leaning back, "you want to play Kit Carson to our John C. Fremont?"

"Meaning?" I said, though I felt what was coming.

"Yeah. Guide Gewald to Hawthorne's Hole and Hogue's Flats and other far and unexplored places. Sorry I can't be the chief scout. Not today."

"It's a waste of time, I bet, but sure, if you want me to."

"It's not so much I want you to as the show's got to go on. He's the state, remember, and local authorities find themselves baffled, plumb baffled. Two men done in and none jailed. Action is called for."

I said, "I guess."

"We've got some time, Jase." He got extra effect by adding, as if as an afterthought, "Time enough, even if I've caught sight of the stripes of the invisible skunk."

"You have!"

"Yup. But no evidence. Nothing convincing except to me. So I'm not telling yet. So we have time for Gewald."

"I can keep a secret."

He found a slim cigar, lighted it slowly and drawled, "We-ll."

I knew then he was going to tell me a story. With action called for, he was going to tell a story in the cowpuncher language he used in such cases. Yet he wasn't wasting time, not in my book.

"Time was," he said, while making sure the cigar burned all around, "there was two old-timers in my town, both hearty for their years and able-bodied except, as you might say, their love muscles had petered out on 'em."

He paused, smiling, though he might have known I got the drift.

"That was a shame for a fact, seein' as both of 'em had had enough women to stock two harems apiece. Like Casey Jones in the song, on the four-posted bedstead they won their fame."

He paused again, letting the story take shape in his mind.

"One of them codgers was Herman Bamberger, who still shod horses off and on, mostly just before the county fair when people raced their quarter horses. You know the kind. Early foot but not stayers. The other old-timer was Gene Zimmerman, who collected his welfare check and counted it welfare enough.

"They was pards, more or less. Gene used to come around to the blacksmith shop and sit on a block and watch Herman tackin' on shoes. They was pards mostly on account of age, I reckon, for Herman was a sour old bastard whereas Gene was a smiler. Different makeups. You got to remember that."

Having laid the scene, Charleston took two slow drags on his cigar. I waited.

"One day a studhorse with some years on him, who was still pretty good on the track but better yet as a sire, was brought into Herman's shop to be shod. Gene was there looking on.

"Well, sir, about the time Herman was gettin' a front shoe nailed on, the stud pushed out a yard or so of workin' joy prong. It interested Gene, bringin' back memories, I reckon. When Herman let the foot down, Gene said, 'Look,' pointin' to how the stud was dingin' his dong on his belly. 'Don't that just make your mouth water?'"

I was supposed to laugh, of course, and I did, but not too much, feeling, as Charleston's age and beginning-to-gray hair came to my mind, that what was funny to both of us might also be rueful to him.

"That ain't the point I was makin'." Charleston's words, still cowpuncherish, jarred me away from my sympathy. "Not the point a-tall."

"No?"

"No. Herman took a look at that eager pecker, and what he said was, 'I would nut the son of a bitch.' That's the point. End of story, too."

"And that's a clue?" I asked.

"Think it over."

I was thinking it over when I went to feed and water Mrs. Jenkins' chickens. Who—no, whom—did the story point to? Everybody at first blush, for no man really liked it that another had more than he did, whether in money, brains, virility, automobiles, girl friends or baseball. Whether in anything except piety probably, though even there there seemed to be some competition. No use thinking about Buster Hogue, my first choice if he hadn't been laid to rest, for he was kind of a head-pounder, meaning he was tempted to hammer down sprouts if they pushed up high enough to rival his standing. Junior Hogue might take after his old man, though I had my doubts. Simp Hogue was a no-no. That left Professor Hawthorne, Dr. Pierpont, Guy Jamison, who were as unlikely suspects as the shirttail characters we'd interviewed. Nothing I could see there. Sheriff or no sheriff , story or no story, my mind kept going back to the Hogues.

The chickens attended to, I looked up Terry Stephens, who was out of a job again because an inconsiderate rain had doused the forest fire he was fighting. We played catch. My arm, warmed up, felt strong and good, though I kept Terry chasing after wild pitches. Our team had lost while I was taking Mrs. Jenkins to her new, happy home. Score, 9 to 5. No team was going to score nine runs off of me, unless I walked the men in—which seemed possible.

On the stroke of one o'clock I was back at the sheriff's office. Gewald showed up a few minutes later, and we drove away in Gewald's state car after Charleston had wished Gewald good luck, knowing he wouldn't have any.

Gewald looked like a hell's-fire, ganted-up preacher bent on sniffing and snuffing out sin. He was dressed in a dark suit, wore a dark tie and on his head had a hat clamped and dipped down in front in the manner, if not of preachers, then of cattle buyers, prods in hand, poking their choices out of a corralful of steers. His coat, opened, revealed a belted six-shooter.

His mouth had no fun about it. If it ever smiled, I thought, it must have been at the sight of a hanging. A dedicated man, he was, and some words of the sheriff popped into my head. "Beware of dedicated men, Jase. They'll push dedication clean to destruction, all because they're so right."

"First thing," Gewald told me as we started to wheel, "I want to see that professor along with his dolly." He shied me a glance and snorted, "And what the hell are you doing with the baseball?"

I answered, "I don't know how good you can shoot," to which he snorted again.

I directed him onto the gravel road. By this time I had a jolting acquaintance with every rock in it. What with all the official traffic, I thought, the county and state ought to pave it, counting the cost against punctured gas tanks, flat tires, broken tail pipes and other dear benefits of the wild.

The county weed-cutters had been along, though, so's to show people that their tax money worked, and

the smell of snipped and torn growth came good and
sharp to my nose. The sun was a high kindness today,
and a breeze sifted our dust away. I could have enjoyed
myself, alone or in other company. We scattered a
covey of young prairie chickens. Gewald ran over one.
Dedication didn't jibe with delay.

At the late Ben Day's mailbox Gewald braked,
seeing the name, and got out and thumbed me to do
likewise. He asked me where we figured Day's killer
had hidden. I couldn't be certain, now that the brush
and grass had been mowed, but I showed him as well as
I could. He began poking and moving the downed
growth, but it was me, not really looking but just idly
scuffing, who saw the shine of a cartridge. I picked it
up. It had been fired. It read .303 SAV.

Gewald said, "What? Give it here."

Having no standing, I gave it.

He studied it and put it in his pocket, rasping,
"Huh. Just like the first," and led the way back to the
car, mission accomplished.

It happened that Professor Hawthorne and Geet
both were at home—which might have been rated
lucky. They came out of the kitchen door as we drew to
a halt. Her hair, drawn back from her forehead, fell
loose down her shoulders. That's all I saw of her
immediately, her face and the hair drawn back and
rippling, for a couple of lines from Lewis Carroll ran in
my head. She wasn't a child but still—

> *Child of the pure, unclouded brow*
> *And dreaming eyes of wonder!*

"Of course, sir," Professor Hawthorne was saying
after introductions, "we will help in any way we can.
Come in, won't you?"

He took us into that pleasant lodge room and saw
that we were seated. He wore a long-used corduroy
jacket and pants but looked trim as ever. For a silly
moment I fancied his Vandyke must have been guaran-
teed perpetual care when the Lord first plotted it out.

In character, Gewald kept his hat on, though it

seemed to me all heads should uncover in the presence of Geet.

Gewald started, "I am here, Professor—"

"Please, not 'professor.'"

"All right, Mr Hawthorne. I am here, as a state investigator, because there has been no local progress, none whatever, toward the solution of two cowardly murders. I hope to determine the guilty party or parties, no matter the failure so far."

"I see," Hawthorne said. "You are taking over the case, then?"

"That is too much to say. I am helping or, if you please, leading the investigation."

"I wish you success. But a good many of us, most, I daresay, have faith in our sheriff."

Gewald nodded shortly. "Of course. Of course. A good man, but there's a saying about two heads being better than one."

My father would have answered, "Even if one is a sheep's head."

"Yes. I have heard that old saw."

Gewald didn't show he found any sarcasm there. He sawed on. "A few questions then, Mr Hawthorne, by way of clearing the undergrowth. I am given to understand that you had your troubles with the late Buster Hogue?"

"Not troubles, Mr. Gewald. Mere differences, and those laid aside. Sheriff Charleston has my report. Surely you've seen it. I have nothing to add."

"He had to tell me, having failed to put it on paper. I'll assume he was accurate, if not professionally thorough."

"A safe assumption, I'd say."

"More interesting to me," Gewald said, "is the three-oh-three Savage you report missing."

"Begging your pardon, not what I report missing but what is actually missing. Is and was."

"It hasn't shown up?"

"No. I would have notified the sheriff."

"Yes. I suppose," Gewald seemed to agree. "Now don't you find it peculiar that the rifle is missing, was missing while one murder, then another, was done?"

"Of course. Odd indeed."

"The guilty rifle, you might call it?"

"I hardly see how its guilt can have been established in its absence."

"Circumstantial but to me convincing enough. Especially—"

Gewald interrupted himself by getting up. He reached into his pocket and produced the casing I had found at the mailbox. "What do you make out of this?"

"No more, even less, than you. I already knew about it."

"Not this casing, Mr. Hawthorne. It is the second we've discovered and, like the first, came from a three-oh-three Savage."

"May I ask where you found it?"

As Gewald hesitated, maybe thinking he alone had the right to pose questions, I broke in. "It was close to Ben Day's mailbox, Professor Hawthorne, right where the sheriff and I thought the killer had hidden." I couldn't resist adding, "I found it myself."

Not until after I had spoken did it really strike me that Geet and I had sat as outsiders, as mute listeners to a dialogue that was polite but all the same prickly. She shied me a glance of what might have meant appreciation—which Gewald didn't.

We were all silent for a minute. Then Gewald said, "The guilty gun. Two casings from same."

"May I say again," Hawthorne asked, his beard a little thrust out, "that it has not been established from what gun the cartridges were fired? And who can say, at the present stage of investigation, that the same rifle fired both of them?"

He was right, of course, but, it seemed to me, just technically. One .303 rifle missing. Two .303 cartridges fired. Q.E.D., but not to him yet. I wished he wouldn't be so professorish.

"You may say what you please, Mr. Hawthorne," Gewald answered. "You might also quit quibbling if you are as eager as I to determine the culprit or culprits. Understand, I am not accusing you, not of anything. I am not even suspicious, except as I am suspicious of everybody involved. But I insist that the circumstances are funny, 'funny' meaning peculiar, 'funny' meaning open to suspicion."

"It's you who are funny!" Geet's voice rang clear in the room, reminding me of the bell sound of a metal triangle tapped to bring the hay hands to supper. "Doubting my father, whom you don't even know!" The pure, untroubled brow was not untroubled now. I didn't admire it the less. "It's your privilege that he's even willing to talk to you."

"Hush, Geet," Hawthorne told her. "He's only doing what he believes is his duty."

"And making a mess of it." Her unfriendly eyes turned from Gewald to me, still unfriendly.

"Mess or no mess," Gewald answered, not fazed at all, "I want to see your assortment of guns, Mr. Hawthorne. I want to see where you kept the Savage until you reported it missing."

"To be sure, Mr. Gewald."

Hawthorne got up, unlocked the big cabinet and showed his prize rifles. The collection didn't interest Gewald very much. His concern with history went back only as far as Buster Hogue's death.

"And now, if you'll follow me," Hawthorne said.

The two walked out of the room, leaving Geet and me there.

"Why did you have to bring that person here?" she asked when they were out of earshot, her eyes still unfriendly. "That person!"

"He represents the state," I tried to explain. "There was nothing else for it."

"Who determined that?"

"Sheriff Charleston. Look, I can't pick and choose . . ."

"He could have come himself."

"Other fish to fry, so he told me."

"Some vote-catching clambake, I suppose."

"Now look here, Geet. You can't fault Sheriff Charleston to me."

"Tell him hello from the suspects."

While we talked, the telephone in the kitchen had been ringing, shorts and longs and combinations, in the way of many-party lines. Now, abruptly, she came from her chair, graceful as grace itself, said, "That's for us," and hurried from the room.

Her brow was less troubled when she returned. She took her seat and sat thoughtfully. She even smiled, but more to herself than to me, I suspected. After a while she said, "You'll have to forgive me, Jase. I got upset. You're all right."

"I'm glad something changed your mind."

"You're all right, I say again, you and your baseball and your trust in the sheriff."

Gewald and Professor Hawthorne came back to the room, neither looking as if a peace pact had been signed.

Gewald said, "Come on, kid."

I followed him out.

CHAPTER SIXTEEN

"Hogue ranch," Gewald said after he had planted himself behind the steering wheel.

I gave him general directions and added specifics when necessary.

"Your professor," he said once we had begun to rattle over the rocks. "Niggling high-toned talker, or didn't you notice, being under hypnosis?"

I ignored the dangler he tied to the question, not wanting to bring Geet into the conversation. "You didn't do so bad yourself," I said.

"Three years of law school," he answered.

"Oh."

For a minute he was silent, then went on as if the explanation wasn't explanation enough. "My father was a minister. Educated man. Knew right from wrong. So do I."

I said, "Oh," again.

"I found out the law is a liar, and I quit it."

Mr. Dedication, I thought. And to understand all was to forgive all, but my forgiveness was limited to a balky respect for his single-minded rigidity.

"Sings hallelujah, any lawyer does, if he can win a not-guilty verdict for a guilty defendant. Brags, 'I sprang him,' when he turns loose on society a sinner against it. Venal, dishonest profession, the law."

Gewald rolled down the window and spit and was silent, presumably giving the law more of the same in his mind.

We crossed the bridge west of the picnic grounds, passed the turn-off to Old Man McNair's place and wheeled on.

The mid-afternoon sun was beginning to blaze, but the day was still good. A breeze from the west brought the scent of pine with it, and the mountains rose gaunt and beautiful, blue against the blue sky. From this elevation I could see the whole valley sweeping southeast and beyond it the free roll of the plains. Badger Clark's lines contrasting east and west came to mind,

Such as they never could understand
The way we have loved you, young, young land.

What was more, Jase was all right—after one telephone call. My hand tightened on my all-right baseball.

We swerved to the left at my direction. A half-mile ahead, in a mown meadow where haystacks stood, lay the Hogues' ranch house and outbuildings, part of the latter screened from sight by the house. Some scattered cows gazed curiously at us, and one of them in the manner of cows decided to cross ahead of us at the last minute and came close to becoming a casualty.

Gewald braked to a halt in front of the house. It was a sprawling, old-fashioned building to which age and size and rude taste had given an air. A roofed, deep verandah ran across the whole front of it. Out of the car, I could hear the cackle of hens and the soft *blat* of a calf. Behind the house someone was pounding, the sound coming clean and sharp like metal on metal.

At Gewald's thumbed order I went to the door and knocked. Junior Hogue's wife opened it, looking too hot to touch after a session over the cook stove. She was a fat, tidy woman with clear, honest eyes.

"You'll find Junior and Simon both in back," she said with so little shown curiosity that I wondered if solitude and hard work had not filed the normal bump down.

Followed by Gewald, I went around to the back. Junior and Simp were setting a new post for a corral, Simp holding and Junior shoveling and tamping the dirt solid around it. Near them on the ground were a hammer and a bucket of spikes. Both men, stopping work, looked up without any word of welcome as I approached.

I introduced them to Gewald and said, "Mr. Gewald is a state criminal investigator. He's here to find out who shot your dad."

Junior stared at Gewald, his heavy face reflecting suspicion. Simp wasn't talking. Junior said, "What's the matter with the sheriff? His job."

I answered for Gewald, who just stood, sizing the two up. "The state thinks the sheriff needs a helping hand."

Junior said, "Huh," as if the matter had been considered and dropped.

Gewald spoke now. "Surely you want to find out who killed your father." The words were as much question as statement.

Junior reversed his shovel and tamped with the handle. Between tamps he answered, "Smart thinkin'."

The sun got a clean shot at us there in the open. A bead of sweat ran a clean furrow down Junior's grimed face. Simp toweled his crotch with his pants. Gewald must have been hot, suit coat, revolver and all, but he wasn't sweating. I wished for a cold drink.

"Simon," Junior said, "see the post's straight."

Simp changed its angle.

Out of somewhere—outbuilding or field—a big

dog came barking. He lay down panting before he could take a bite out of me. A horse thrust its head out of the half-door of the barn and let out a whicker. A good horse, it looked like. All Hogue horses were. Simp, holding the post, stared at the animal, almost as if hunting a communion there not to be found among humans. Junior kept on working.

"I'd like to ask you some questions," Gewald said.

"Ask 'em."

"Here in the sun? While your attention's divided between me and that posthole?"

Without a word Junior let the shovel fall. Before he moved off, he said to Simp, "I'll be back in a shake, Simon."

Gewald told him, "Better both of you come."

"You're invited, too, Simon," Junior said, then turned to Gewald and added, "But you lay off him. Hear? He don't know anything."

That last remark, I thought, had a wider application than Junior intended. If Simp knew anything, it was about a world unseen by other eyes, though in his own eyes now flickered the shadows of misgiving, as if strangers had invaded his realm.

Junior took us around to the wide verandah and motioned toward seats. There was an old glider there, plus a rocker and a couple of straight-backed chairs. Simp took the glider and, like a kid, began swinging. Gewald moved a chair around so's to half-face him. I sat in the rocker, it being the only seat left. I could hear Mrs. Junior back in the kitchen, getting well done along with whatever she had in the oven.

"Simon," Gewald began, "just a couple of things that may help us. Don't be alarmed, boy."

"I told you to lay off him," Junior said.

Simp swung and, swinging, started a conversation no one could understand with someone nobody saw.

"A couple of questions can't hurt him," Gewald answered to Junior.

"They better not."

"Simon," Gewald said then, "do you have any

idea, any idea at all, how your father met his death?
How he might have met it?"

Simp, on the down swing, gave Gewald a wide
stare and stared away. "Ho," he answered almost in a
shout and resumed his private, untranslatable talk.

Junior said, "He met his death from a bullet."

"Hell, I know. Simon! You, Simon! What do you
know, what do you suspect, about the death of your
father?" Irritation was putting a keener edge on Gewald's
saw voice.

Simp slowed his swing and finally stopped it. He
looked at Junior as if asking help, a lost child asking
help.

"If he doesn't know anything, how can he say
anything?" Junior asked. In his face I thought I could
see a thunderhead forming.

"He understands, and you understand he understands, and, by God, as the son of the slain man you
ought to cooperate."

"I would, if you knew your ass from third base."

"I know enough to know when a man's faking. He's
faking."

"The man is nuts, Simon," Junior said, too quietly.
"Don't be afraid."

"The question is simple. So can the answer be."
Gewald had softened his tone, then went back to hard
stroke. "Simon! Answer me! Any idea who killed your
father?"

For a minute Simp wrenched his eyes to the real
world. They flowed with fear. It struck me he might fly
away, like a bird, into the refuge of heavens he alone
knew. He said, "No idea, have we, Junior? No notion at
all. Eh, Junior?"

"You're mighty right, Simon," Junior answered.
"No notion at all."

Assured, Simp burst out in talk, not to us, not in
our language.

"Shut up, Simon, and listen!" Gewald's voice cut
through the gabble.

Simp shut up, his short assurance lost, his fears
returned.

"Did you have it in for your old man, Simon?"

It struck me that Gewald had forgotten the constitutional guarantees, forgotten them in his hard purpose and heat. As the thought struck me, Junior jerked forward in his chair and said, "Jesus Christ!"

Gewald took a fresh breath to power his saw. "Did you kill him? Simon, did you kill him? Want to talk in a jail cell?"

It wasn't fear now but pure terror that swam in Simp's eyes. He leaped from the glider, jumped from the porch and ran around the house yelling.

In that same moment Junior sprang up, plunged at Gewald and swung at his face. The chair and Gewald went over.

Gewald clawed for his six-shooter. I got it first while Junior stood over him—a big man dazed by the punches of circumstance.

Gewald climbed to his feet. His mouth leaked blood. He said to me, lisping, "Arrest this man!"

"No."

"You have the gun."

"Not the authority."

"Obstructing an officer in the pursuit of his duties. Give me that gun."

I held it behind me and said, "No," again. The officer in pursuit of his duties might have counted among them a pot shot at Junior. I added in the pursuit of peace, "Don't hit him any more, Junior."

There was no real need for that last. Junior's rage had been shot with the one blow. He said, "I got to find Simon. He's scared crazy, my own brother is."

"You'll have to come in to the office, Junior," I told him.

"I will. I promise I will, just as soon as convenient. I got to get Simon calmed down."

"Promises!" Gewald chimed in, his speech thick. "From a man like this one!" Blood was dripping down his chin. He didn't notice.

"I said I'd come in, Jase. That means I will."

"Good enough. Good enough for Mr. Charleston and me."

Junior jumped from the porch and disappeared. I could hear him shouting, "Simon. Oh, Simon. It's only me. Junior."

Gewald said, "Shit," and at last wiped his chin, and that was the mood in which we went back to town. Shitty.

CHAPTER SEVENTEEN

"Well, how's my short-peckered friend?"

It was morning of the next day—mid-morning because I had slept late again—and the speaker was one Mike Day. He was just coming out of Old Doc Yak's office, his big face split in a smile that suggested he had just sold the map to the legendary Lost Dutchman mine. Behind him was Doc Yak, looking pleased, too— which wasn't his habit. Ordinarily it was as if he couldn't take time for a smile on account of all his concerns, two of whom I could glimpse in the waiting room waiting for him to finish his facial experiment.

"Late for work," I answered, and then asked of Doc, "How's Mr. Gewald?" Gewald had dumped me off when we returned from the Hogue ranch the night before and had charged into Doc's office to get repaired.

"Needed a stitch or two," Doc Yak said through the smile that showed he was a little long in the tooth. "That was all, not counting dental attention."

I signaled a quick good-bye but, though my sudden idea called for speed, didn't run to the office. Mike Day, I thought. Yep, that Mike Day would bear some investigation.

And Sheriff Charleston for sure would be at his desk at this hour. He hadn't been last night, either early or late, and so hadn't got my report about yesterday.

When I went there, Halvor, left alone in the office, had told me, "He's gone to the big city again, with company or without. Take your pick." His imagination was making him grin.

"Know what took him there?"

"Why, now, I imagine it was wheels, saddle horses bein' more or less out of date."

"So's your wit," I said and went home.

Later, so important did I think the day's happenings, I tried to telephone Charleston, tried five or six times, and lagged off to bed at midnight with Mabel Main's words in my ears. "How in hell do I know his whereabouts? Because I'm a telephone operator? Get yourself under the feathers, Jase. That's probably where your big boy friend is." Maybe the sour note of disappointment had come into her voice. "Whose feathers I wouldn't guess."

I fell asleep still wishing I could make my report.

Now, at 10 A.M., Charleston was in the office but not at his desk. He was standing at a window and answered to my good morning with an absent-minded, "Hi, Jase."

Jimmy Conner was on the phone. He hung up, got up and said, "Kid locked in a bathroom." He left, taking with him a jimmy and a bunch of keys.

"That damn Mike Day," I said, taking the first opportunity to alert Charleston.

"Yes," he answered, not turning from the window.

"We ought to inquire about him."

"So?"

"Look here, Mr. Charleston," I said to his back. "It could have been this way. Mike went to collect the debt from his brother. That would be the strange car that Guy Jamison saw. So the brothers got into a fight over the debt, and Mike shot Ben. Then he took out fast, let a little time go by, and came back, saying he had just heard about Ben's death. What he wanted, what he wants now, is to be appointed administrator of the estate. That way he'll collect the money he loaned and probably something to boot."

Charleston turned now, his smile small and thought-

ful. "Could be, Jase," he said. "If you can make other
things fit, then we've got a case."

In my fit of inspiration I hadn't thought about other
things, such as where the body was found, the tennis
shoes, the trail in the grass, the new Cadillac that
Jamison would have identified. But still and all?

"Mike Day won't be appointed administrator,"
Charleston was saying.

"Why not?"

He was a long time in answering, as if my question
had to work up through an overlay. "He's got a record
in Minnesota. His license plates led me to it. Record
enough to deal him out. Some swindle, some shady
dealings in stocks. Fine and six months probated."

"And still at it! You can almost bet your boots he
just made a sale to Doc Yak."

Again my words seemed buried, or, rather, to
enter no more than the fringe of his thought. He
answered absently, "I reckon Doc Yak's old enough to
take care of himself. Job for the county attorney anyhow."

Charleston sat down and frowned. "Damn it, Jase.
It has to be. There's no other answer. But to prove it,
to get other people to see, there's the pinch and the
bind. I need a tool."

I couldn't give him one even if I knew more, so I
said, "Could I ask where is Gewald?"

"He got to me early and told about yesterday. Now
he's gone to the city for dental work." He added with
the smile that meant sour amusement, "Didn't trust our
local practitioner."

"But he'll be back?"

"Sure. Chompin' with his new bridgework. I fought
a delaying action this morning, his teeth and I did, but
he's out to get Junior. He'll bring charges. Assault.
Obstruction. Grounds enough, too. He might even
push for an information charging murder or murders,
mad as he is."

"If he's still as mad as he was yesterday."

Charleston breathed out a slow breath and drew
another one in. He spoke as if idly. "I could tell him
about Buster Hogue's hat."

"Why?"

"He might get bamboozled by it and held up for a spell."

"Bamboozled?"

"Like we were. The hat doesn't signify, hole or no hole. It's one of those little things that stands big in the way of progress. Devil's work, Jase. What does it matter whether Loose Lancaster saw Buster Hogue take his hat off before he was beaned in his bald spot?—which he didn't and that's no matter, either. He saw the hat lying away from its perch after the shot and got mixed in his dates. Hell."

The sheriff swiveled away from me and then swiveled back, as if determined to put his mind on what I had to say. "Now tell me," he said.

"I couldn't report last night, not with you gone some place."

He didn't answer. He merely nodded.

"Well," I went on and told about yesterday, all that I could remember, which, I was sure, left out nothing important. The telephone rang a couple of times while I was talking, as it did again later, but the matters seemed trifling though Charleston made note of them.

When I was finished, he said, "Deductions, if any?"

"For an innocent man Simp Hogue seemed too scared."

Charleston put in, "For an innocent, sane man."

"All right, but what's more, Junior Hogue shielded him. Didn't want him questioned. Didn't want him to answer."

"To you, then, they're suspect, one or the other or both?"

"I don't know. You asked how things hit me."

"Of course, Jase, and thanks. Good report. Now let's go back."

We were interrupted by Jimmy Conner, who came in carrying the jimmy, the keys and grub for the one guest the law had invited to jail. "Kids," he said, as if being young was a capital crime. He rid himself of the keys and the jimmy and took the grub to the back.

Then Charleston asked, "Why do you figure Ben Day was killed, Jase?"

"Because someone had it in for him."

Charleston smiled a sort of fatherly smile. "You can do better than that." It struck me that he was being indulgent.

"Blackmail," I answered from a sudden enlightenment that embarrassed me because it had been so late coming.

"Right. Victim or victimizer?"

"Far as I know, Ben Day didn't have much."

"Right again."

"Where does that get us?" I asked, knowing almost before he replied.

"Closer. It rules out the peedads. Who but the damn tax-gatherers would try to get money out of Loose Lancaster, Oscar Oliphant, Pierre Chouquette, Old Man McNair or the likes of them? That leaves?"

"It sure as hell leaves the Hogues. Junior's got a bankroll now his father is dead. I hear there's a trust fund for Simp."

"Yes. Who else?"

"Guy Jamison, I guess, and Professor Hawthorne, I guess, and Doctor Pierpont, I guess, but I don't guess it's any of them. Might as likely be Old Doc Yak or Felix Underwood or you or anybody, except they weren't at the picnic." I was getting mixed-up and out of the mixup asked, "But did they have to be at the picnic?"

"You mean, did he have to be? As my old granny used to say, put your thinking cap on."

"Affirmative," I told him, pleased to have hit on a term so professional.

He nodded, dismissing the subject, and asked out of left field, "How far along is the report you've been writing?"

"Pretty far."

"Bring it up to date, today if you can, and let me see it."

"It's not filled out like I want it. It's mostly what people said, plus just an idea or two of my own. I aim to get it in better shape sometime," I said, feeling shy about having him read it although I hadn't put anything very personal or intimate in it.

"That's what I want, what people said."

"Could I ask why?"

"Pisswillie, Jase. I'm a rube sheriff, as Gewald would tell you. Don't take notes except in my head. Not often, I don't. And what I put there may get blurred, not being written on parchment with indelible ink. Confirmation. Correction. Addition. Reminder. They're what I need. And you're just the boy that can do it, too, as the old man said to the Lord when praying for relief from his piles."

"All right. I think I can finish by night."

"I'll be here. Get along."

I fed the damn chickens again before going home. They had adopted me, the fool birds, forgiving the swing of the guillotine in the light of my handouts of grain. I thought, as they clustered clucking around me that, if ever I beheaded another, it would be out of necessity. Yep. For good nutrition, good-bye trust.

I worked all that afternoon and into the supper hour on my report. Now that Charleston wanted to see it, it had to be accurate, down to the crossing of t's and the dotting of i's. Mother interrupted me just once, saying as she put down a plate of fresh cookies, "What in the world, Jase? A whole book you're writing?"

"The whole truth," I answered and thanked her and kept on working

It was the edge of dark, or a little later than that, when I handed my account to the sheriff. Halvor was on duty and, seeing my tome, said, "Sherlock Holmes rides again."

"I saddled up for him," Charleston replied, his tone sharp, for him sharp. "Halvor, I'll be here till all hours. Why don't you take the night off? But keep in touch."

Halvor seemed so pleased at the prospect that he appeared not to notice the suggestion was a dismissal. I watched him as he went out, a big, good-natured man with a self-reputation for wit, a fondness for women, and a well-known generosity of heart.

Charleston riffled my pages and then began reading. I waited, five minutes, ten, maybe more, seeing him bob his head now and then and now and then hearing him say, "Yes, yes," to himself.

The phone rang, and I answered it. Mrs. Kindrick, who owned six no-account curs, was calling to complain that one of them had been poisoned. Thank heavens, he was recovering, but still and all it was the sheriff's job to catch poisoners, wasn't it? I acknowledged as much and promised our vigilance, thinking so doggy a woman maybe ought to buy some strychnine of her own.

To the sheriff's inquiring gaze I said, "Kindrick dog poisoned, but not enough."

He answered, "Hum-m," and went on reading and by and by said, "Jase, a damn fine report. With your consent I'll take excerpts from it right now, and you might as well go on home."

He didn't, and I didn't, for at that moment Junior Hogue entered with a gun in his hands. He looked, I thought, desperate, though it was hard to read that heavy face.

I kept my eyes on him and the rifle and hitched my tail to the edge of my chair.

He walked to the desk, swung the gun, butt foremost, to Charleston and said, "I found it."

"A three-oh-three Savage."

"You asked if we had one. There it is."

Charleston began examining the rifle, which looked old and beat-up, saying, "Sit down, Junior," as he proceeded.

"What's more, I told Jase here I'd come in," Junior continued. "You got a charge against me, ain't you?"

It came to me then that Junior was not desperate in the way I had feared but, rather, moody and muted, his usual loud mouthiness reduced by the worry of circumstance.

Charleston levered open the breach of the gun. He answered, "Not yet, Junior. Maybe soon. Maybe tomorrow. We stalled it so far." His gaze didn't come up from the gun as he added, "Did I tell you it was a three-oh-three Savage that killed your father and also Ben Day?"

"I could guess at it."

"And you went looking?"

"No. I just happened to see it in the toolhouse, stacked up with some old axles and junk. I was searching out Simon after that state man—what's his name? Gewald—scared him crazy."

"Simon knew where it was?"

"I don't know." The question put new wrinkles in his coarse face. "But Simon wasn't hidin' in the toolhouse. And I tell you he wouldn't—"

"Hold on," Charleston said. "To find answers I got to ask questions. How did Simon and your father get along? What was their relationship?"

Junior sighed and shook his head and moved in his chair. "The old man was mighty disappointed in Simon. He tried hard to bring him up to scratch, you know, puttin' out good money, plenty of it, for that phony head-healer. I guess he—the old man, I mean—couldn't help showin' how let down he was with my brother."

"And you acted as the buffer? As Simon's protector?"

"You would, too," Junior answered, as if defending a position some might have thought womanish. I almost began to like the big lug.

Charleston asked, "Did they quarrel?"

"Simon don't quarrel. He just whoops and talks crazy or goes quiet and draws into himself. That, or he runs away. Dad scared him."

"You and your father quarreled, huh?"

"Sure. Mostly on account of Simon. But neither of us ever thought about killin' the other. Christ sake!"

Charleston had not only looked at the rifle, from butt to muzzle, but he had sniffed at the opened breach and put a scrap of white paper in it and had sighted down the barrel for wear and burned powder. Now he said, "Bad shape. Loose breach and worn rifling."

"Once it was used hard, I guess," Junior replied, "but for a long time it's just been layin' around. We never fired it."

"Someone did, Junior. Someone did recently."

"It wasn't us." Junior's rough voice had risen a notch. "Here. Let me see."

A smell at the opened breach was enough to bring out of Junior, "Oh, Jesus!" He handed the rifle back.

As he sat there, silenced and looking bewildered, Charleston said, "I think you can help us, Junior."

"How?"

"Let us take your fingerprints."

"That's crazy. They'll be on the rifle. You know I've handled it."

"All the same, I want your prints. You've given me an idea, Junior. I been wanting a tool." He turned. "Jase, your printing kit here?"

By good luck it was. As I moved to get it, Junior was saying, "I don't get it, but all right. But don't try to take Simon's prints. Not guilty—he isn't—and, besides, you'd scare him shitless."

"Not Simon's, then. I don't want to scare him."

Junior let me fingerprint him. For an amateur I did pretty well.

When I had finished, Charleston said, tapping the butt of the rifle, "Keep things to yourself, Junior, but, you see, this isn't your gun."

CHAPTER EIGHTEEN

Charleston was out of the office when I arrived there next morning after fighting a wind that came close to sweeping me into its stream of torn branches and gravel and weeds and discarded containers. Halvor was on hand, though, answering the phone when it rang and otherwise reviewing his prowess while he considered adding scalps to his coupstick. That's what I guessed, anyway.

The phone rang two times. Once, Halvor told me, it was Mrs. Durton calling to report a case of indecent exposure. Otto Dacey again, who exposed himself only to pee and not always then, but what could you do, besides scold, with a man declared sane?

"Yes, Mr. Gewald," Halvor said when the phone rang again. "No, sir, he's not in right now. Yes, right soon, I expect."

Jody Lester, our part-time stenographer, came in and laid some typed sheets on Charleston's desk, sighing, "Overtime," as she did so. "Your sheriff has no regard for the poor working girl."

Halvor had plenty of regard, though. He showed it as she switched out of the office. Then he said, reverting, "The state gets some rare sparrows, Sherlock. Even I could do better, I bet, than Mr. Gewald. Even old Jimmy. Even you that the sheriff has somehow took under his wing."

He lighted a shorty cigarette—no filters for him— and gave me a queer look. "Damn funny about you," he said. "If I didn't know the sheriff so well—"

"Use your head!" I answered, feeling blood climb my face. "It's simple. If he used you or Jimmy same as he uses me, the other one would be on night and day duty, both. That, or he'd have to put on an extra man which the office isn't budgeted for."

"Dumb kid," he said while the thought percolated. "Yeah. Anyhow, the baby is his and yours, the killin's, I mean, and it's all right with me, seein' the baby is such a bastard."

Charleston came in then, grinned a hello, his teeth showing white in his wind-reddened face, and moved into the private office. I followed, thinking he might want me to. On the flat of the desk there were my report and a few pages in his handwriting that I imagined were excerpts from my deathless prose. In a corner stood the Savage. From a drawer he took Junior Hogue's fingerprints, which Junior himself had signed.

While he looked at them, studying some other matter, I asked because the bare possibility nagged at me, "You don't think Junior was playing it sly, bringing the gun in?"

"Forget it. No ruse. His father might have. Not Junior."

"He seemed to think the rifle was his, sure enough."

"He did, Jase, and it wasn't and isn't—and that fits the scheme. You care to take my fingerprints, boy?"

I thought, "What in hell, now?" but walked into the main office, got Halvor to move, and took out my kit. After I took his impressions, he signed a name, not his, to them. The name was T. A. McNair.

"Now yours," he said, not explaining. To mine he had me sign Oscar Oliphant.

"I might pick up a couple more, just for effect, understand," he said as if all were plain to me. "Maybe some true ones, so's to satisfy truth and my conscience." He grinned, the grin deepening the lines around his mouth that weather had worn. "Thrice armed is he who's halfway honest."

While we cleaned our hands, I said, "I don't get it."

"You will," he answered. "Maybe. Maybe. Long shot. Like shootin' over a hill or around a corner. Changin' the figure, it might come out in the wash if we can get it to wash."

"When?" I felt entitled to ask.

"Can't say, Jase. Let's go out. I went shy on my breakfast what with one thing and another."

"Gewald's due in," I told him.

He made a small face and gave a small shrug. "It won't hurt Mr. Gewald to wait."

Outside, the wind caught us. It was like a hand in the face or a push on the back, depending. For a space I turned hind end to it so's to let my lungs breathe, and Charleston yanked his hat hard on his head. Low over the mountains the wind clouds drifted, the clouds that mothered the winds of the world. The sun shone, the upper sky was bright, but from the west came the screech and assault of torn air.

We were in front of the Bar Star when here came Gewald, forging ahead as if neither gloom of night nor wind of day could stay him from the completion of his appointed rounds. He wore a light overcoat which blew heavily at his sides.

He halted and gave a rasping hello to the wind. His lip was still angry, and a tooth looked as if it had had just repair enough to last him to the next service station. "What've you done?"

"Investigated," Charleston answered. The words, spoken loud, had been torn from them and borne east to far-away flatlands, and now he added, "Can't hear myself think." He opened the door of the Bar Star and motioned us in.

No one was inside except the bartender, Smoky LaFrance, and Otto Dacey, who looked at us from the height of his certified sanity and went out to let the wind blow him—which was just as well.

We were hardly seated at a table, hardly had time to refuse drinks, than Gewald asked, "You bring Junior Hogue in?"

"Didn't need to. He came in by himself."

Gewald let out, "Ah-h," indicating satisfaction. "Now I can squeeze him." He opened his coat and leaned back. "He's holding back on us, you can bet."

"Think so?"

"Never a doubt. I'll squeeze it out of him."

"When and where?"

"Right away. In the county jail." He came forward and studied Charleston's unrevealing face and asked as if he couldn't believe what might be the answer, "You held him?"

"No."

"Assault! Impeding an officer of the law! And likely a key witness in two murder cases! Yet you didn't hold him. Why in hell not?"

Charleston said without heat, "The complaining witness wasn't on hand."

"Good God! I've met a lot of sheriffs in my time—" A shake of Gewald's head finished that sentence. "All right. I'll go out and get him myself. The kid here better steer me again."

I said, hardly believing I said so, "Not this kid,"

and thought I saw a glint of approval in Charleston's eyes.

Before any of us could go on, the door opened and let Junior Hogue in.

Gewald's voice sawed out a soft, "Ha-a."

Junior walked to us and, ignoring Gewald, said to Charleston, "Sooner or later, probably sooner, you told me. You want me now?"

"Yes, by God!" Gewald's bruised lip gave his saw the hint of a stutter, as if the blade had been flawed. "You're coming with me."

Junior still ignored him.

"Any difficulty, I'll snap the cuffs on you." Gewald flapped his overcoat, making a jingle. His revolver was in sight on his hip.

"No," Charleston said, his tone contained. "He won't do that, Junior."

Gewald scraped back his chair, like a man making ready to rise. "Some things I won't put up with."

"Same here." Charleston's voice, still quiet, had an edge of held anger in it. "By law I don't know that I have to put up with you."

"Common sense makes the rules."

Junior was looking from one to the other now as if bewildered that he, a wanted man, had raised such a row between two men of the law.

"I'll go on my own, Charleston," Gewald continued. "No thanks to you, as I'll sure God report." He paused as though to find the right pitch. "And now, Mr. Sheriff, you can't keep me from filing charges against this man, this Junior Hogue."

"Nope. Suit yourself. No cuffs, though." Now Charleston bent over the table and fixed Gewald with voice and eye. "But I'll tell you this, Mr. Gewald. Once arrested, Junior Hogue will be released on his own recognizance to appear for trial at a later date, later than might be to your convenience and liking. You can think about that."

Gewald's mouth opened, obviously to his hurt for he was quick in closing the gap. Between tight lips he said, "If you weren't an officer of the law, I'd suspect you had put a fix in."

Charleston gave him a grin with no humor in it. "As an officer of the law, I'd suspect you were right."

CHAPTER NINETEEN

There was one thing or two that I did know, more that I didn't and at least a couple beyond guesswork accounting.

The sheriff didn't want the Hogue brothers pushed, not now, anyhow, and, as Gewald phrased it, had put in a fix to keep Junior Hogue out of jail. But why? A belief in an innocence more important than the guilt of assault? A hunch that, with freedom, the Hogues would betray themselves? The first guess was the likelier, I figured, though for myself I couldn't dismiss the unwelcome feeling that Junior or Simp Hogue or both were involved in the killings.

The business of fingerprinting, and where could it get us? Sure, there would be prints on the rifle, just left by Junior and Charleston, and possibly older ones which, though, an amateur like me couldn't lift. I filed the deal under the head of ridiculous, suspecting it wasn't. I could understand, or, rather, imagine why Charleston had asked Junior and me not to blab about finding the rifle. Simple: What the guilty party didn't know could hurt him.

Why had Charleston gone to the city those two nights? Not to entertain a date, whoever she was, I felt sure, or not just for that reason. I passed.

What excerpts had Charleston taken from my report, and why? Pass again.

What would I do with Mrs. Jenkins' chickens? Go

on feeding them until the last ancient died of the roup or the pip and so closed down the rest home? There was enough grain on hand to nourish them into fat middle age.

Today was Friday, two weeks and a day from the night of Buster Hogue's shooting, and on Sunday I was scheduled to pitch. My arm felt as rusty as an abandoned pump handle—which seemed not to matter much, considering the general state of affairs.

The general state of affairs, represented by one item, stuck sore in my gizzard as I wandered down the street. Less than an hour ago Charleston had dismissed me, saying, "Take the day off, Jase. Go fishing, or warm up your soup bone for Sunday's game. See you another day, boy."

I went, the words being orders, and, walking, chewed over the dismissal and, in addition, his behavior preceding it. He had had Jody Lester in the office that morning and had dictated to her for a solid hour and in that time worked down and through his neglected if unimportant correspondence. The last letter was from a lady named Charleston who wrote from Miami wanting to know, among other things, if he was related to her or to a missionary who had distinguished himself by getting killed in the Congo. She had found the sheriff's name, she said, through a sister-in-law, a grassroots writer on politics, who had paused at our courthouse last summer while touring.

At the finish of his dictation Charleston had got rid of me. Fine thanks for my services.

Mike Day was coming out of the bank and called to me as I passed by, "Hi, you, boy." He approached and asked, "What's new?"

"Nothing."

"Too bad," he said and went on, his big face momentarily clouded. "We got poor Ben put away, and for the present I'm staying at the ranch. A financial sacrifice, too, but a man does what he must."

I wondered when he would learn the estate wasn't his to administer and how he would act then. But it was none of my business, nothing was, and the hell with him anyway.

"To change the subject," he said, "I have a suspicion the sheriff's on a cold trail, that is, if he's on one at all."

"So."

"The way I figure it, Ben made enemies not just outside but inside of prison. One of his old pen pals, so to speak, could have come to the ranch and done him in. No way to tell who."

"Sounds neat," I answered, "but how come they met at the mailbox, how come Ben had on sneakers, how come all that?"

"Where's your imagination, kid? Let's suppose, using the mail or the telephone, some old enemy dared Ben to meet him." The usually smiling face had gone severe, as if the mind behind it saw circumstances as they had been. "Now the man, whoever he was, wouldn't want to have it out with Ben in front of Marcy Belle and the kids. Hell, no. They'd be witnesses. So the man dared Ben to meet him on the road where the mailbox is at. Can't you see it, kid?"

"So far."

"Ben wasn't one to take a dare. Don't you believe it. Though he didn't make it this time, he always figured he would come out on top, one way or another, overhand, side-arm or underhanded. That's why the sneakers and that's why he sneaked."

An old, held-in hate showed naked for a minute through the bland shine of his eyes. "Apologies to my mother, but Ben was, always was, a low-down, sneaky son of a bitch."

"You got a theory, all right," I said.

Mike Day drew a breath and fixed a smile at the end of it. "Sorry, kid." The eyes turned innocent as onions. "Talk too much, but it's something you might think about."

I thought about it, walking along. I thought about Mike Day in particular, Mike who could explain how it all happened. The strange car that Guy Jamison saw could have been one that Mike rented and later returned to the place where he'd left his Cadillac.

It could be, but other situations argued against my telling Charleston, who would probably dismiss my suspicions again.

Felix Underwood stood in the door of his funeral parlor, waiting for business. He asked me, "Ready for Sunday?"

"No. Seen Terry Stephens?"

"Working out on a ranch, so I hear."

I went to the Commercial Cafe for a Coke. I was the only live one there, if ten cents makes a live one. I looked in the Bar Star, for nothing, which is just what I saw.

At home I gathered up three worn baseballs and threw at my old barn-door target, threw hard too soon and had to shag a bunch of wild pitches with an ache in my arm. Then Mother called me to lunch.

My father lighted his pipe after we'd eaten and, sizing me up, said, "You seem out of sorts, son."

"Yeah."

"What's the trouble?"

"The sheriff's cleared the decks, and me along with the clutter."

My father considered and said, "I see," and blew out a wondering breath of smoke.

Mother put in, "I don't. Why would Mr. Charleston do that?"

"I believe you clear the decks for action, Mother," my father told her.

I said, "That's my guess, with me out of it."

"If you mean danger," Mother said, "then the sheriff's right. You stay out of it."

"But I don't want to." My voice had risen. "I'm not going to if I can help it. Don't you see? Can't you understand? I've been in on the case since the beginning and be damned if I'm shuffled out now."

Mother said, "Son."

"All right. Son this and son that, but I'm old enough to know what I'm doing!"

My father said, "We hear you, Jase. Please don't

yell. Just tell us what you propose to do if, in fact, what you suspect is true, If the sheriff says no to your presence, what can you do? Or we?"

"No is no," Mother added, her face drawn with an anxiety I didn't appreciate.

"I'll find a way," I said.

My father kept puffing his pipe. His words came out along the stem. "I have every confidence in Mr. Charleston." He took the pipe out of his mouth and his eyes away from the smoke. "Also, son, we have confidence in you and good reason for it." He turned to Mother. "It may be, my dear, that we overdo the business of thinking of Jason as our little boy. Mothers incline to do so and fathers, too, I suppose. But he's almost eighteen, soon subject to the dratted draft."

Mother began to cry. Through her hands she said, "Please!"

"Compared to what may face him soon," my father went on, "what is this small episode? And in view of his age has he not the right to some choice?"

"Not if the sheriff has his way," I said.

"I am coming to that. I will write Mr. Charleston a note. It will give our permission for you to accompany him. More than that we can't do."

He wrote and signed the note, and Mother signed it protestingly, and I left home full of heart but did remember to kiss my mother, who said in my ear, "Oh, do be careful, my son." I thought of my mother as love and my father as sense but not with the full appreciation that was to come to me with the years.

The question was whether to show Charleston the note now or later, at what might turn out to be the decisive moment. I decided on later and so loafed around town, making frequent excursions to the courthouse to be sure that the Special was still in its parking space.

Not until along about four o'clock did I enter the office. Halvor had come on duty early, and Charleston was reading a book, *The Immense Journey,* which sounded like some kind of adventure story. He looked up from it to say, "I thought you were taking the day off."

"I thought maybe I would write more on my report," I answered, hopeful he would take stock in my lie.

He gave me a hm-m and returned to his book, and I walked into the private office. My report was there but not the excerpts he had hand-copied. The Savage stood in a corner. I picked it up and looked it over. It was a working model with a steel butt plate, stamped SAVAGE QUALITY above and below an Indian-head outline which together constituted the trademark. A good light rifle, though discontinued. A good rifle once. Why hadn't the most recent user run a cleaning rag through it? Why hadn't Junior?

I listened for the ring of the phone, suspecting Charleston was waiting a call. Why else sit there in office hours reading a book? Twice, when the phone did ring, he answered at the first buzz. One call, I gathered, was from Monk Fitzroy, his out-of-town deputy, and was no more than routine. Apparently the second came from a householder who had just discovered the fridge had been raided. I heard Charleston mutter, after he had hung up, "Damn town needs a town marshal."

I waited, rifle in hand, doing nothing.

Then the phone rang again, and Charleston said, "Yes, Mabel. Thanks. Remember, under the hat," and there was quiet again.

And still I waited, waited until I heard Halvor go out to get grub for a couple of offending drunks who would be released once they'd paid their hangover penalties. Then I couldn't wait any longer.

Charleston glanced up. "You still here?" he asked me as if I shouldn't be.

"Still here." I added, feeling brash, "Waiting, like you."

He smiled then, but yet as if to dismiss me, and said, "Reminds me somehow of a maiden lady in my old town. She swore she wouldn't die wonderin', but she was sixty-four at the time and died two years later and left the rest of us wonderin'. Maybe that's us, Jase, forever wonderin'. Now, boy, clear out."

But the phone jingled again, and Charleston seized

it and listened and said into it, "Good. Good. And
thanks. I'll see you shortly."

He got up then, full of purpose, and told me,
"Jase, I reckon I'd better borrow your fingerprint kit."
From a drawer of his desk he was pulling the prints
already taken.

"Sure," I answered, "but borrow me along with it.
Aren't I your print man?"

"Sorry, boy."

"But wait! Look here!" I brought from my pocket
the note signed by my father and mother and handed it
over. I knew by heart what he was reading:

> *Dear Sheriff Charleston,*
>   *Reluctantly, but at his insistence, we agree*
> *that our son, Jason, may accompany you in*
> *your investigations if you want him to, this*
> *with no risk or liability to yourself or the*
> *county. For us to deny him, we feel, would be*
> *wrong in view of the strength of his senti-*
> *ments. With faith in your judgment.*
> > *Sincerely,*

Charleston frowned, reading it and for a long minute afterward, and my breath blew shallow. He said, "Oh,
goddammit, Jase, nothing's going to happen, nothing
violent and maybe nothing at all except I might make a
fool of myself."

"Yes, sir," I answered and held up for his decision.

"All right, then," he said finally. "But you stand
aside. Hear me? Completely aside all the time. Take
your baseball along and don't interfere."

It was plain enough that he wasn't pleased, but I
answered gratefully, "Yes sir. I promise. I do."

I got my baseball and kit, and he took up the
fingerprints and for an instant seemed to think of
buckling on the six-shooter that hung on the wall but
voted against it. Halvor came in with the prisoners'
grub as we were about to take off. Charleston told him,
"It's all yours."

It wasn't to my surprise that he turned off on the

rocky-assed road again, for I had come to look on it as a flyway, which birds of the law and other assorted fowls followed.

The wind of yesterday had long since blown itself out, and we jolted along to the blessing of a sky without clouds and a lowering sun without blister. It was hard to think that hereabouts in such peace and quiet, with the ribbon of the river winding along to our left and the grand rise of the mountains ahead, murder had been done. There was plenty of time for such observations, for Charleston said not a word all the way.

It was to my surprise that Charleston turned into the Powell Hawthorne place, but I didn't comment or question. If he wanted to play mummy, let him. I would stand aside, as ordered and promised.

The friendly dog greeted us, and Geet came out, her hair touched by a whisper of breeze, and gave her hand to Charleston and then to me. Her face had that clean, open, somehow pitiful look that had struck me before as both invitation and warning. "It didn't take you long," she said, smiling.

Charleston was carrying my kit and I my baseball, and he answered, "Hi, operative. Thanks."

She led us into the lodge room, where Professor Hawthorne rose and shook hands, his welcome moving his beard. "So you've located my rifle," he said as a statement of fact.

I had thought the .303 was a secret, shared only by Charleston, Junior and me, but I kept silent as befitted a stander-aside.

"And I am led to suspect—but won't guess—that you have a suspect," Professor Hawthorne continued.

"Unnamed," Charleston told him, speaking from his chair with a little wave of his hand. "Right now we hope you'll let us fingerprint you."

Professor Hawthorne took a long time in answering while his eyes measured Charleston. Then he ventured, seeing or knowing more than I did, "For verisimilitude, I would imagine."

Geet said, "Meaning the appearance of truth."

"Have it your way," Charleston answered, his grin showing his teeth. "Also, a man feels supported if he has some sure-enough facts underfoot. What's more, a public servant has to act even-handed, else he'll get kicks from behind if he's wrong."

"Ah, yes," Professor Hawthorne said. "By all means take my prints."

"Jase."

I took the kit and did the best job I could, and while I was doing it Charleston sat back and talked. "Our office isn't much. Not up to date. A haywire operation by modern standards. No real communications system. No lab at all. We just bungle along."

"Muddle through, the English would say," Geet threw in.

"The 'muddle' is right, the 'through' is questionable," Charleston replied. "Underfunded, every bureaucrat complains, but underfunded we are. Otherwise these murders, maybe—" An outward wave of his hand completed the sentence.

"Not by Mr. Gewald," I dared to put in, speaking for almost the first time.

"There are few substitutes for horse sense," Professor Hawthorne said. "Without it, what use are systems, electronics, computers?"

"I think Father is betting on you," Geet told Charleston. "Faith is the word."

Charleston, always discomfited by praise, hitched in his chair. "Thanks, but I've never seen it move a mountain."

I was done with the printing by that time, and we, meaning Professor Hawthorne and me, proceeded to clean up.

Charleston got up and looked out the window and then consulted his watch. "Time to go, I guess, Jase. Oh, but first, Mr. Hawthorne, will you sign your name to the prints?"

I put my stuff together and saw through the window that the day would soon fade off into dusk. We were six weeks or more past the solstice but still in the time of long twilight. It would be an hour, maybe more, before a man could distinguish a star.

Outside, Geet said, "Good luck. Let us know."

Charleston answered, "Why, sure," and walked to the car, the fresh prints in his hand.

It was my day for dumb astonishment. Just short of the river bridge Charleston turned right, toward the small patch of land owned by Dr. Ulysses Pierpont. No trespassing signs, big, red and newly erected, introduced the trail to his trailer house, which was parked close to a stunted jack pine and seemed as alien to its surroundings as a painted igloo. Dr. Pierpont came to the door and, seeing us, jumped down the steps and charged out as if to give the boot to invaders. Then, recognizing us or the Special, he held up.

Charleston commanded me, "Remember, you stand aside." He pushed out of the car, the whole collection of prints in his hand, and I trailed off at an angle. What breeze there was carried a good smell from the door, like potatoes frying with onions.

Charleston said, "Good evening, Doctor. Hope we're not interrupting your supper."

Dr. Pierpont returned the greeting, not mentioning supper. He stood waiting, a picture of cool and competent professionalism even in an unbuttoned shirt and old slacks. From the west the half-sunken sun shed a red glow.

"We need your cooperation but won't keep you long," Charleston said. "You see, the murder weapon's turned up, the one that killed Hogue and Day, and it happened to have some good fingerprints on it."

"Is that so?" Dr. Pierpont answered in the tone of a man who believed that it wasn't.

"Yep. Lots of metal on a Savage three-oh-three. Butt plate, lever and trigger guard, breach housing. The man was careless or else thought our dinky office couldn't lift prints."

"What has that to do with me?" Dr. Pierpont asked.

"For all I know, nothing, no more than with all the others. I'm taking fingerprints from everybody around.

Routine for me, so the county will have some excuse for my wages." He fanned out the fingerprints. "See. Here's Buster Hogue's prints, signed by himself, and Old Man McNair's and Guy Jamison's, and just now I took Mr. Hawthorne's, signed by him, too."

Dr. Pierpont said, "Nonsense."

"Probably so. It would take a miracle to match up any prints with the prints on the rifle." Charleston paused and said in another tone, "All the same, I want your prints, Doctor."

Still the cool and capable professional, Dr. Pierpont answered, "It is an insult, an insult to my known standing and to my profession, an insult to me as a person."

"But you don't mind, Doctor?"

"I object to the exercise of petty authority."

"No compulsion," Charleston answered and went on in that harder, that slow-cutting voice, "but your refusal would look mighty funny. Yours alone. That news would shock the profession."

I thought Dr. Pierpont would continue to balk. He looked at Charleston, his face cold and set like that of a man weighing insults. Then he said, "You give me no alternative. Let me turn down the stove."

It was time to turn it down. I could smell onions scorching.

"I'll bring the kit," Charleston said to his back. He made for the car, waving me off as I started toward it.

Then two scenes appeared, right and left, and grew into one. Charleston came from the car, the kit in his hand, and Dr. Pierpont stepped from the trailer house, an automatic pistol in his.

"Get off my property!" Dr. Pierpont said, moving the pistol for emphasis. "Get off, you and your boy!"

Charleston halted. "Are you out of your wits?"

"I recognize conspiracy. Get off!"

"What conspiracy, Doctor?"

"You're paid by it. Wealth. Arrogance. Power. Position." The words came out distinct, separate, charged with cold certainty.

"Like Buster Hogue's?"

"I said get off!"

"Like Ben Day's?"

"Not Ben Day. Get!" Dr. Pierpont lifted the pistol.

"By God," I heard Charleston say, "if you're not a madman!"

That one word burst on me, like daylight seen when a blind is jerked up. Madman! The body fixed, steady in purpose, and the voice controlled but with ice in it, the ice of conviction, of righteousness, or certain grievance. The automatic, pointed, didn't waver.

I knew Charleston wouldn't retreat. He would walk into that gun. And I knew Dr. Pierpont would fire.

Charleston took a pace forward. The pistol fixed on its target. And I stood there helpless.

"I don't miss," Dr. Pierpont said. "It seems you have noticed."

Then my hand felt the ball, waking my mind. No time for a windup. Rear back and fire. I aimed for the head. The ball went wide. It hit the gun and the gun hand and knocked the hand down but left the gun in it.

This much I saw as I ran. I swung for the jaw. The pistol jerked around and met my fist. It went off.

Then, deafened, slammed back and down, I scrambled on the ground and rolled free and saw Charleston, on his knees, strike at a face already bloodied. He struck again.

I heard myself cry out, "Sheriff!"

It was with a wrench, like breaking out of a spell, that Charleston left off, picked up the loose pistol and climbed to his feet. Dr. Pierpont didn't move. He was out.

"All right, Jase?" Charleston panted.

"Maybe singed just a little."

"He could have killed you, and, son of a bitch, I told you to stay out of things."

There was anger in his voice yet, and I answered, "Yes, sir."

Then he smiled the smile that was never far from his face and touched my arm. "You're a good boy, Jase.

Thanks." He turned his eyes down on Dr. Pierpont. "I was afraid," he said, "that he would go through with it."

"He sure God meant to shoot you."

"Not that, Jase. The fingerprinting. If he had let us take his, where would we be? Big bluff, ours, but he broke."

At the sheriff's direction I got a dipper of water from inside the trailer house and doused Dr. Pierpont. It was in doing this chore that I found my right hand was hurt.

We handcuffed the prisoner and put him into the car. From the back seat I held his automatic on him, though I didn't think he would act up, being shackled and only half-conscious to boot.

We were near home before Dr. Pierpont began to show signs of revival, and then Charleston told him, "Medical treatment first, Doctor. I'll see to it."

Dr. Pierpont didn't reply.

"Now if you want to tell anything, tell it, though you're not obliged to. If you want an attorney, you're entitled to one."

"I want to see Doctor Phillip Phillips," Dr. Pierpont answered at last.

"Well sure, but you're not hurt much, and Old Doc Yak's pretty competent."

"I said I want to see Doctor Phillips."

"All right, but where's he and who's he?"

Dr. Pierpont replied, "He's my psychiatrist."

I could almost hear Charleston saying to himself, "Well, pisswillie." I did to myself.

CHAPTER TWENTY

Dr. Phillip Phillips was a large, silver-haired man who looked a little saggy, as if the troubles of his patients had overweighted him during the years. He was pretty much what I had expected to see, but didn't, in the person of Dr. Ulysses Pierpont. Right now, seated in the sheriff's private office, he appeared maybe sadder than usual after a long session with Dr. Pierpont.

Present in the private office, in addition to him, were the sheriff, Gewald and I. In a corner rested Charleston's recorder with sixty minutes of tape on it, put there for my benefit. I sat with my right hand plastered and bandaged, thanks to Doc Yak, and my wing in a sling. Dr. Pierpont occupied a cell in the rear, which Jimmy Conner kept visiting in the interests of rare-sparrow science.

"This is a depressing case," Dr. Phillips said while we waited on his report. "A disappointment, a failure on my part."

Charleston answered, "I'm sorry, Doctor. You have a name for it, I suppose?"

"Names," Dr. Phillips said slowly. "What are names except convenient handles for mixed bags of troubles? Even when used professionally, I avoid them when I can."

"So did Doctor Pierpont, or so he told me."

"Yes. He was both my colleague and patient."

"Patient?"

"That should cause no astonishment, Sheriff. Many men, most perhaps, enter the profession because their own mental and emotional experiences have been severe. Often we psychiatrists go one to the other for assurance, guidance, even therapy." Dr. Phillips gave us a tired smile. "In hospitals for the tubercular many of the personnel have been afflicted with the disease." He sobered again. "My failure was the failure to recognize the extreme nature of Pierpont's illness. I thought he had only a mild megalomania, if I must use a term."

Gewald spoke now. "And instead?"

"It was, it is— No. First, let me say that I am speaking because I feel that I must, if only in the interests of Doctor Pierpont himself. More, he has no objection though convinced that I'm wrong. The illness was and is, then, true paranoia. It is difficult to detect, as well as rare, because, except in the direction of his delusion, the victim is rational and mingles with society unsuspected. He is also chary of proclaiming what he is certain is true, for to him spies exist, unknown but many, and, more, he can hardly afford the reputation of crackpot. Nevertheless, he sees plots against him. He sees classified if undeclared enemies, united though dispersed. Conspiracies are as real to him as the hand in front of his face. Conspiracies by Communists, by fascists, by blacks, by whites, according to the set of his ill mind."

"And by the establishment?" Charleston asked.

"By selected members representative of it, if that is his way."

"How come?" Gewald asked.

Dr. Phillips spread his arms in a hopeless little gesture. "Sometimes we find out the why. Sometimes we think we do. Sometimes we go wrong and sometimes despair. What goes into the shaping of a personality? Doctor Pierpont was born into a large and underprivileged family. For an education, for his professional degree, he had to struggle every step of the way, often to the accompaniment of gibes, of derision by those who through circumstance felt superior to him. It is easy to say that a malignant resentment against wealth and authority and standing abides in him as a result. It is easy to say envy. It is easy to say his own felt inadequacies in the presence of equal or better men force him, in self-defense, to extremes, to an absolute belief in conspiracy. I suspect these explanations, though not without force, are too simple. But there is no need to go deeper now. In his mind conspiracy is established."

Charleston motioned with a dead cigar. "And no getting him out of it?"

Dr. Phillips leaned back and put his hands in his lap. "I don't know. Once I spent hour after hour with a paranoiac. It was Communists he saw, not men of position or riches, Communists behind every bush, in every little circumstance, and himself the prize and sole quarry. I couldn't change him."

"Does Doctor Pierpont own up to the killings?" Gewald asked.

Charleston, I was sure, could have answered the question but let it pass.

"Oh, yes," Dr. Phillips said, "I'm sure he will admit to the physical facts, but, in a sense, you won't get a confession. Instead, you will get an assertion of proper and inescapable conduct. He won't disclaim his acts: he will justify them." The doctor paused and then said with sad emphasis, "He believes."

Gewald ground out, "Not guilty by reason of insanity."

"Confession or not," Charleston said as he put a match to his dead cigar, "we have other evidence. A box of three-oh-three cartridges cached away in the trailer house. Two missing. A man in the city who can identify Doctor Pierpont as the buyer. Clerks remember rare sales."

"All right," Dr. Phillips said, sighing. "Now, Sheriff, would you tell us what made you suspect him?"

"After a question. Was Doctor Pierpont successful in his practice?"

"Well, more or less."

"Meaning less than more?"

"I wouldn't say that, not quite. He was engaged by the state, you know, part-time at Central State Hospital."

"And that was important to him?"

"Fifteen thousand dollars a year."

Charleston nodded and took a drag on the cigar. "Now for my part, huh?"

"It would be interesting to me."

Gewald said, "Me, too. But leave me out of it. Seems I was barking up the wrong tree." Then was the first time, I believe, that I saw him smile. It was a rueful smile, but a smile.

"If you need a fill-in on the characters, stop me," Charleston told Dr. Phillips.

"I think I'm sufficiently informed."

"The sequence is easy to follow, once you're on to it," Charleston said. "Accept it that Doctor Pierpont was offended by Professor Hawthorne and at the same time felt sore as all hell at Buster Hogue. So he stole

Hawthorne's rifle and used it on Hogue. But Ben Day had seen him and got into the act by attempted blackmail. End of Ben Day. At the last, as a final trick, Doctor Pierpont planted the Savage in the Hogue toolhouse."

Charleston paused and addressed Dr. Phillips. "He may be off his rocker, Doctor, but he played plenty foxy."

Dr. Phillips nodded and said, "As I would have expected. No contradiction there."

"It was safe enough—the stealing and planting. The Hawthornes never lock doors, and the Hogue toolshed is set off a piece from the house."

We sat silent, all of us, waiting on the sheriff's next words.

"The night of the picnic, Doctor Pierpont fired from the ridge, snaked down the hill, no one watching but perhaps Day, and dressed Buster's head. Nice cover-up and no loss to his purpose since he was mighty sure Buster would die."

"That's a plausible construction of events," Dr. Phillips said, "but what I'd like to know, if you please, is what led you to suspect Doctor Pierpont."

"Yeah." The sheriff sighed as though he weren't enjoying himself, though I imagined he was. "The field was open at first because everyone, most everyone in the canyon and roundabout, had had his troubles with Hogue. Then Ben Day got himself killed, and it narrowed the pasture. I got to thinking, not so much about motive, but just what kind of a man our murderer was, and my mind galloped off to a remembered, funny affair in my old hometown." For an instant he was silent. "But I guess I won't tell about that."

Dr. Phillips said, "Do, if it's at all pertinent."

So Charleston spun the story, with appropriate embroidery, of the two old codgers that were worn out and the studhorse that wasn't. He ended on the note struck by the blacksmith who would have castrated the stud.

A glint of amusement and a longer look of respect

showed in Dr. Phillips' eyes. "Not exact," he said, "but illustrative nevertheless."

Charleston offered cigars to everybody but me and lit one himself. "Back to business," he said. "Day's murder—that's if he was trying blackmail—cut the number of possible suspects to four, for only four in the field could pay more than a few bucks at most. They were the Hogue brothers, namely Junior, Professor Hawthorne, Guy Jamison and Doctor Pierpont."

Gewald smiled again and shook his head. "And me, I picked the Hogues."

I thought I could say, as a sort of comfort to a man who might not be so bad after all, "I kept on suspecting them, too. But I couldn't keep Mike Day off my list, either."

"They were possibilities," Charleston said, "but Mike Day didn't fit as a murderer. Too outgoing a person and too smart. And the circumstances in his case were unlikely to boot. As for the Hogues, you had to take into account that the Hogues were and are a close family. Quarrels, yes, I suppose, but respect and protection for each as blood kin. I couldn't believe either of the sons had shot the father, though Doctor Pierpont had said in words that were guarded but all the same pretty sly that Simon, the simpleton, was capable of it.

"Guy Jamison and Professor Hawthorne I dismissed right away. Hell, Jamison is too busy for feuding, and Hawthorne has too many honors, is too much established, for envy or grudge. Besides, neither is the type for planned violence."

Dr. Phillips smiled faintly. "A rather risky assumption, isn't it, Sheriff?"

Charleston smiled back. "Sure is. Anyhow, there I was left with Doctor Pierpont and no shred of evidence." He fingered papers that lay before him. "I had to convince myself. I had to enforce my suspicions. And Jase here has kept a record, a good one, of what was said and done in the case. These are passages from it. Shall I skip through them, maybe putting one with another as I go along?"

"Please," Dr. Phillips replied.

"All right." Charleston shuffled the pages. "First off, Doctor Pierpont tried to buy land from both Buster Hogue and Professor Hawthorne. The Hogues laughed at him—and I don't suppose he can endure ridicule."

"He least of almost anyone," Dr. Phillips said.

"Professor Hawthorne turned him down, too, in different words and a different manner. From an interview I had with him later I judged he found both replies arrogant. That's a word of his, 'arrogance.' More than that, I have it from Miss Marguerite Hawthorne that he left their place—shall we say?—in a huff. She said—it's down here in Jase's notes—that he suffered from delusions of the illusion of grandeur."

Charleston looked up from the pages as if to allow for comment, but nobody had comment to offer.

"So back to the interview that Jase and I had with him before he murdered Ben Day. It sounds innocent enough, until added to that gun-muzzle gaze of his and that sober mouth, when he says that everybody, worldwide, needs therapy—which is what he said and which means mental therapy. He says Buster Hogue got disgusted with him and so terminated treatments for Simon."

Again Charleston's eyes left the pages and came to us. "They must have had a row over that, and anyhow you can bet your boots that Doctor Pierpont felt insulted down to the raw."

He sifted through the papers and, doing so, added, "Buster Hogue was a loudmouth." He found what he wanted. "Now here, referring to the doctor, Junior Hogue called him a fake. Where else but from his father did he get that idea?"

None of us answered.

"But you don't have to imagine a row or Doctor Pierpont's hurt feelings," Charleston continued, changing pages again. "Here's the slant on the doctor. He said this when we talked about Hogue: 'Men of means often assume the mantle of superiority.' Those are his words, and he went on to say, 'I meet a good many of them in my practice. All psychiatrists do.'"

He cocked an eye at Dr. Phillips, who answered,

"True enough. Often we are regarded as menials. We have to take care lest the attitude warp us."

"Then Doctor Pierpont made mention of wealth in some hands. I asked if he didn't mean wrong hands." Charleston consulted his notes. "Here's his answer: 'Where so much of it is. Wealth, and consequently position and influence. Consequently a circle of toadies, too. Power misplaced.'"

After a pause Charleston added, "Wrong hands, I would bet, meant any hands but his own."

"Not quite," Dr. Phillips put in. "His own hands wouldn't be the only exception. Include the empty hands of others. He would identify with them, perhaps only so long as they remained empty, though even there there could be exceptions."

"Right, Doctor, but, you know, looking back, I think I almost had him when he talked about wealth, influence and power. A little more, and he would have jumped the reservation. He caught himself just in time. But, man, was he dead serious about that one subject!"

Charleston leaned back, his hand leaving the pages. "Have I satisfied you, Doctor?"

Before Dr. Phillips could answer, Gewald broke in, his rasp of a voice sounding incredulous. "And that's all you had to go on?"

"Slim pickin's, sure enough. Oh, a thing or two more. I called Doctor Pierpont to ask if he could do anything to help in a sad case of senility. Old Mrs. Jenkins' case. He said he couldn't, which isn't the point. The point is he seemed to lack any—what's the word, Doctor?—compassion." Charleston came forward, then pushed the pages to the center of the desk for anyone to see. "In addition, according to Jase who was there, the hired hands at Central State Hospital liked Doctor Pierpont just fine. Not so with his peers, as they say. Not so with the medical men. They didn't like him, and he didn't like them. That's the impression Jase got."

Now Dr. Phillips answered Charleston's question. "Yes, I'm satisfied." He thought a minute and gave a sad grin to the sheriff. "Your talents, it would appear, transcend those of detection alone."

Gewald broke in. "I give you credit, Charleston, but tell me a tail end or two. How did Pierpont get to Ben Day's?"

"Hired a car, one that Guy Jamison saw. His own car was too showy."

"I figured so. And how did you know he'd be at his place when he was?"

"Our telephone operator, Mabel Main, kept calling his office, changing her voice, on the pretense of making an appointment. It wasn't hard to find when he would be out of town."

Gewald began shaking his head. "I can't believe, Sheriff, that you've given us all your evidence, which adds up to no real evidence at all. There's not a solid piece in it." He looked up inquiringly.

"I had only one solid piece," Charleston answered, "and I was a slow poke in seeing it. But here." He brought the papers back to him and shuffled.

When he had found his place, he went on. "When I telephoned Doctor Pierpont about old Mrs. Jenkins, I happened to mention we'd had a second murder that day. He asked who and I told him, adding just a bit or two more of what we knew. Now I'll quote what he said:

" 'I don't envy you your job, Sheriff. No clues yet, I suppose. Two shootings and no clues.' "

Charleston's eyes went to our faces and settled on Gewald. "I didn't tell him Ben Day was shot. I didn't tell him the way of the murder."

Gewald considered. "I see. But it could be argued he would assume Day got shot, since Hogue had been."

"A stronger assumption is that an innocent man would have asked the how and the why and the wherefore. No, he betrayed himself there."

Gewald nodded. "I said before I give you the credit."

"Give luck the credit. In the beginning, and for a good part of the way, I acted on hunch. I just felt Doctor Pierpont was guilty. Say my hunch was right, I didn't know if he wore gloves while using the rifle. Would he figure, if he figured at all, that our jerkwater outfit couldn't lift prints"— Charleston shied a glance at me—"which it can't yet? Nothing to do then but try a big bluff, and it worked. Luck."

Dr. Phillips shook his head, then said, "But there must have been an additional something, some incident or circumstance, some fracturing factor that impelled Doctor Pierpont to violence, to the ultimate violence of murder."

"Oh, there was," Charleston answered. "This I found out in the city last week, from the head of the state Board of Charities and Corrections."

"I can guess," Dr. Phillips put in, nodding his sad head.

"Yes. Buster Hogue was trying to get Pierpont fired from his state job. With his political weight he had more than a fair chance to do it."

Gewald said, "I be damned."

CHAPTER TWENTY-ONE

There's nothing to do now but round up the strays, as Chick Charleston might put it.

Dr. Ulysses Pierpont insisted on a trial, contending he was as sane as the next man or saner, but at a preliminary hearing it was ordered that he be taken to Central State Hospital for further examination. He subsequently was committed to the place permanently or maybe just until that far day when he finds his lost marbles. For all I know, he spends his time envying the fellow patient clothed by Hart, Schaffner and Marx. I doubt he and Mrs. Jenkins would have much in common.

With the judge's approval I sold Mrs. Jenkins' chickens to Brick's Butcher Shop and deposited the returns with the court. Mother thought about buying a couple of hens, but I put the nix on that, saying I didn't choose to eat off my friends.

Old Doc Yak, who as a doctor of course had no business sense, cleared forty thousand dollars on a five-thousand-dollar investment that Mike Day had conned him into making. The money didn't change Doc, except that it enabled him to buy a new car not half as good as the one that had fallen to pieces.

Mike Day had a good thing, or his company did—rights to coal lands in the northwest that soon came into high demand for strip-mining. He owns the bank now and Ben Day's old place, for which he paid a fair price, as well as a couple of Cadillacs and a bird dog. He has cautioned me against drink and hare-brained financial involvements.

Gewald—now I'm giving credit—had nothing but praise for our sheriff.

Soon after the case of the murders was closed, Geet breezed into the office, fresh as a first flower, her face glowing and her eyes on high beam but not focused on me. She called out, "Chick," and went forward, and I went on out. I should have known. Hell, I did know but had refused to admit it. Those telephone calls and that date, or those dates, with what Halvor said was a dish.

They were married—which, in spite of my knowing, jolted my hormones as well as my notions about sexuality and age. No doubt about it, they got and get along fine.

My feelings have changed, but all I could say to myself at the time was, "Pisswillie."

ABOUT THE AUTHOR

When ALFRED BERTRAM GUTHRIE was six months old, his father moved from Bedford, Indiana, to the town of Choteau, Montana, which had a population of about two thousand. There the boy learned to know and love the high country of the West. His first experience as a newspaperman was working as printer's devil on the Choteau *Acantha*. In 1926, he went to Lexington, Kentucky, and got a job as reporter on the *Leader*, where he stayed for twenty years.

Perhaps the most important event in Mr. Guthrie's career was winning the Nieman Foundation fellowship, which took him to Harvard. There he had time to complete the writing of THE BIG SKY. In 1950, he was awarded the Pulitzer Prize for distinguished fiction.